DREAM SHIFTER

DREAM SHIFTER

...

A novel written by Michael Clark

ISBN: 1523789336
ISBN 13: 9781523789337

ACKNOWLEDGEMENTS

SPECIAL THANKS TO:

Priscilla Jean for the amazing cover art; Ken Burns for helping me make a realistic fight scene; Shane Kennedy for helping me edit the beginning; Richard Romano for continued support and help publishing this book as professionally as possible; anyone that I have talked to about this novel; and finally anyone that purchased my debut short story and plenty more people that have supported my dream with their kind words, interest in my passion, or their cold hard cash.

A note to the person who may or may not have been the original inspiration for the character of *Amy*: I have never loved anyone in my life like I have loved you and I wasn't truly aware of that until I lost you. There are many taboo emotions I could never express to you when we've talked post-breakup. Please remember that due to certain constraints (such as time, plot devices and so forth) I have mixed this character with two other women that have affected me as a person. Also, none of the emotions in this book have been exaggerated and I wrote what I have truly have felt in more than one case. In writing this, I accept that I am ready to move on with a clean slate of emotions, ready to truly devote myself to whomever or whatever comes next. Thank you for playing a powerful part in my life. Without you it wouldn't have been so easy to write out the emotions of sadness and happiness that I have experienced. The emotional spectrum is truly an insane thing. I hope you enjoy the story I have created.

Michael Clark 3/21/2016

This book is dedicated to the memory of my loving father Stephen Clark (1964-2012) and my Mom who is still blessing this world with her presence. I love the two of you more than anything and I would not be the man I am today if not for the two of you. Thank you both, always.

PROLOGUE

WITH HASTENED JUDGEMENT AND A one track mind, Sean Singer rushed to gather everything that was absolutely essential. He smoked one last cigarette in his soon-to-be abandoned apartment. Then he filled a black briefcase up as much as he could, gorging it as if it was an unfed pet. He took his lighter back out and began incinerating a small note. The note was the last physical trace of the combination for the briefcase. Feeling satisfied, Sean dropped the cigarette into an ashtray. He lifted up his suitcase in one arm and the briefcase in the other. Feeling only a little encumbered, he tore open the front door the best he could. Sean jogged lightly through the frigid November weather down the three flights of stairs. Awaiting him was a red Honda Civic. He threw the luggage and briefcase into the back seat. In one swift motion, he turned the engine on and zoomed out of the apartment complex.

He wouldn't miss it there. He lived short-term in apartment complexes like that all over the country. Sometimes for only a few weeks at a time. The nature of his job demanded it. The only thing that was darker than the night sky were the bags under Sean's eyes. Sleep escaped him like a bus he could never catch. Feeling deprived and low on energy Sean lamented not making a coffee before he left. Letting out a deep sigh about the urgency of his mission, he continued on I-90 North for several hours without stopping.

• • •

Ron was laughing at a funny video on his smartphone screen with a twelve pack of Coors Light beside him. It was half finished. Tonight was a regular night for him. He enjoyed the long drives by himself. Ron always thought it was awesome how he got paid to deliver Coca-Cola across a multitude of states. He did this while enjoying anything from an illegally downloaded movie to pornography on his Iphone. Ron thought of his Iphone as his best friend. He'd never admit that to anyone though. His Iphone was always there on his long journeys. The more inebriated he was the more funny and entertaining his videos were. Of course he was *smart* enough to begin drinking after he got past toll booths for bridges and state borders. It was nothing but open Jersey road here. "Hahaha, MAN I love this dang thing." He exclaimed over the sounds of intercourse coming from his phone. Then with a frustrated snort he realized the rest of his video stopped loading. When he looked back up all he saw was a small vehicle's headlights on his side of the road. The last thing he saw was the driver's face on the steering wheel as the Civic came barreling towards him.

• • •

The clock struck three. The collision that ensued was a fireball of red. The interstate was lit up like the 4th of July.

"The unconscious trucker is named Ronald Feinberg of Alabama," stated the first responding officer Jerry Thompson.

"And the other?" Spat out the higher ranked officer who had just arrived.

"Uh. Well, we don't have any I.D. on him but the paramedics believe he was unconscious and possibly even sleeping before the crash. The car belongs to a John Cramford from Des Moines Iowa. He's been missing for a week now." Lieutenant Miles rubbed his temples and spit out some of his chewing tobacco.

"Well, let's get to it then."

Suddenly, Miles' attention was captured by a firefighter pulling a black briefcase from the wreck

PART I
ORIGINS

• • •

CHAPTER 1

JANUARY 18ᵀᴴ, 2020.

IN HIS SLUMBER HE TOSSED and turned as vivid images flashed through his mind. His eyes rolled around under his lids like bowling balls. Somehow he knew it was all mixed up. He saw: A kid with blue hair on his phone, his hands on the floor with a carpet under him darkened by tears, a man watching him on a train. He saw a hospital bed and he flinched, kicking the blanket off his bed without knowing it. Everything was scrambled. Two symbols rose into his mind's eye. He wasn't aware of why they were so important, but deep down inside somewhere he knew that they were the key. The key to what? 火風土水. That was when he awoke.

"Happy birthday!!!" Exclaimed Mrs. Kishimoto as she handed Akira breakfast in bed. "Even though it's your birthday, you still have to go to school," she explained as she kissed his forehead lightly. "You know there's only a few months left."

"Yes Mother," Akira Kishimoto said, despite feeling like he was still in some sort of dream. He let out a large yawn. He opened his mouth as wide as a python would before devouring its prey. Then he exhaled. "And thanks!" His mom hovered with a comforting smile on her face, almost as if she was oblivious to the adult things she could be focusing on right now instead of him.

His room seemed brighter than usual. Even before his mom pulled the curtains from the window to let excess light in. It reflected off of his movie posters and his television set, giving him an extra glare. He was about to grumble at his mom because she was drowning him in light. Then he suddenly remembered the breakfast plate beside him. "I must be dreaming." He said out loud. Then he began assaulting the egg and cheese omelette on his plate.

Checking the clock, he noted what time he had left to shower and get dressed. In the shower he thought of the excitement of the day being a Friday. TGIF. After a few hours of educational torture and the never ending boringness that is senior year; his birthday celebration would begin with his best friends. He was also planning on inviting a cute girl who was friends with his close friends. It was all breathtaking for Akira. Eighteen years old. Not quite nineteen, but pretty darn close. Growing up and adulthood seemed so close that he could taste it...or perhaps his mom just makes omelettes that taste like adulthood and growing up. He had been waiting to be an adult for so long.

He glanced at his mom sipping tea and reading a newspaper. The darkened outline on the back of the paper read: **EVIDENCE IN AUTO ACCIDENT MYSTERIOUSLY GOES MISSING, 1 DEAD AND 1 IN CUSTODY.**

"Bye Mom! Love you!"

"Have a nice day, love you too!" she answered instinctively. And then he was off. Akira wasn't thinking about it at the time, but he definitely appreciated how she woke up extra early to make him breakfast before she went to teach.

Akira spent his day thoughtlessly going through the motions of school, like a zombie that pays moderate amounts of attention in class, rather than eat brains. He was never much of a "try hard" as some kids called it. He was typically saved by his amazing recollection. His memory was practically undefeatable. He barely needed to pay attention, just listen to the spoken information, copy it down and wham! It was stored in his memory banks that he could withdraw from whenever he wished. This came in handy for tests and when teachers asked him questions, usually because they caught him daydreaming. School was not the only front that his memory could be utilized in either, his two prior girlfriends adored how he could remember every single unimportant detail they ever told him. It made them feel good, like they were worth listening to. At most times they were not, as many fifteen and sixteen year-old girlfriends are not.

Akira shyly thanked friends and strangers alike for their "Happy birthday" wishes and comments whether it was in the hallways of the school, or on his own Facebook wall. The occasional teacher would wish him a happy birthday as well. Then they would assign homework. *Talk about irony,* Akira thought sardonically.

After what seemed like decades of schooling, Akira was finally free to go over his best friend's house. Cody was a musician and a hell of a guy. He was always there when Akira needed him the most. Just being in his presence could cheer him up. Cody was having a few people over in honor of Akira's birthday. Akira's apartment was too small and his mom would worry too much about their things and the party goers. They talked about comics and played some video games while waiting for the rest of the guests to arrive.

"So dude, you gonna try to nail that chick tonight? I heard Angela is bringing *her* tonight!"

"Chill man, I don't even know if she's interested. Plus, I would want to, ya know, date someone before we do it." Akira blushed.

Feeling a chill, he got up from his warmed seat on the couch to go put on the sweatshirt he took off when he arrived. Mid-January was still a lot colder than he wanted it to be.

"Cody, you gotta stop trying to live that musician's life man. I mean smoking pot and drinking is cool and all, but you'll never find a good girl that way."

Cody gave a slight roll of his eyes, and started setting up a beer pong table.

"I ain't lookin' for a good girl, I'm just tryna have fun 'till I'm older-then I'll worry about finding a good girl. Until then all I care about is finding a fun one!"

Akira chuckled at that.

Several commanding knocks on the door preceded the clattering of footsteps, as a tan Spanish girl and a blonde entered. Both were physically attractive, almost unsettling by way of their good looks. They were wearing smiles of excitement on their faces, only increasing their friendly aura. Akira recalled how intimidating meeting both of them on separate occasions was, knowing only their beauty at the time. Had he met them both at the same time, he may have even fainted, he mused. But since then he's gotten to know them moderately well, specifically the blonde as she was dating Cody's older brother Jake. Her name was Angela. The Spanish girl who Akira only hung out with twice before, was named Amy.

"Happy birthday Akira!!" Shouted Angela as he felt her embrace. "What she said!" Amy joked, as she gave him the less personal side hug. However, Akira didn't mind because he was able to get within inches of her gorgeous face. She smelled almost as good as she looked.

"Sup bitches?" Cody said, while hugging them both simultaneously.

After the customary introductions were dealt with, Jake finally arrived with a few unknown friends that graduated two years prior. Some other friends arrived, some acquaintances and so forth. Akira enjoyed the party regardless. Him and Cody would go on to best Jake and Angela in beer pong later in the night. His flip cup team would also defeat Jake's team of experienced drinkers.

He high fived Cody. All of this was possible because of Cody and Akira knew it. Inebriated appreciation washed over him. They were the intoxicated kings of the night. Life was good. But life got better when Akira found himself making out with Amy as the clock struck 2 AM. He didn't remember how he pulled it off, nor did he care. Well, maybe he cared a little bit just in case he needed luck again. Her lips were soft and Akira would always think back to that moment and wonder how he avoided feeling intimidated at the time. He just went for it. When their tongues clashed Akira thought to himself that eighteen was going to be a good year for him.

"Wait, what!? -Really?" Akira asked with his mouth wide open, as if he were aiming to try to catch flies.

"Yup." Jake said, half smirking. "Twenty-one. She's even a year older than me and Angela."

"Damn, I hooked up with Jessica McNally last night, but that is straight up impressive bro!" Shot out Cody while stuffing himself full with diner pancakes the next morning.

"I think she asked if I had a birthday kiss and even though I didn't, it technically wasn't my birthday anymore when she did...oh well. I checked my phone when I woke up this morning to make sure I got her number. Even though I butchered her name I did get it!"

"Damn dude, her name has three letters! Let's just hope you didn't butcher her number too otherwise some forty-year-old woman will text you back loverboy!" Cody exclaimed and they all laughed out loud together. Akira decided even if Amy didn't want anything to do with him he was still happy to have gotten that experience with such a gorgeous woman. The more he thought about it, the more out of his league he knew she was.

Akira had no idea of the changes that were headed his way. His dreams from earlier that morning were all but forgotten to him.

CHAPTER 2

FEBRUARY 8TH

AKIRA FELT OVERWHELMED WITH ASTONISHMENT. As freezing cold as the weather was, he still felt warm inside. Only a month had passed since his birthday. In that time he had acquired the girl of his dreams Amy, as well as a driver's license and a car.

"The car is a late birthday present and an early graduation present. Be extremely careful while driving and don't go too fast or drink and driv-"

Akira made certain to tackle hug her before she could finish her instinctual maternal warnings. He was so thankful. The car was ten years old but he loved his "new" 2010 Nissan Sentra anyway.

It was the first responsibility he ever had. Akira never owned any pets before. He promised himself he'd take good care of it. Everything was coming together like a gigantic puzzle, or a shattered vase being glued back together. He had a decent car, only 96,500 miles on it, and even a girlfriend to drive around with.

Amy was gorgeous beyond belief. Her beauty was a bright bulb that never went out. Or one of those joke birthday candles that you couldn't extinguish no matter how hard you tried. They spent one entire all nighter together. He showed her his favorite spot to think and they watched the stars together. And watch stars they did, sometimes in total silence. At other times they were engulfed in eloquent conversation. This continued almost endlessly until the weather proved to be too much. Without consenting his mother first, Akira snuck his new girlfriend into his room and she stayed the night. They romanced a little bit, but he wasn't interested in going all the way yet; and to his relief, neither was she. It was an unspoken feeling that made everything even more special. They spent the majority of the night snuggled beside each other watching Netflix. They even played some board games.

Akira usually did not take advantage of his Mother's trust, but for a girl like Amy, Akira was prepared to defy God himself if it came down to it.

During one of the other sleepovers there was one point in the middle of the night he thought he heard his mom so he awoke. But it ended up being nothing. Instead he smiled and stared at the tan-skinned woman sleeping beside him. She seemed to glow even in her sleep. It was like she was his own personal night light. He managed to fall asleep watching her yet again. He found he was even happier to do this come the second time. When they awoke, he was shocked at how someone could wake up as beautiful as they were when they went to sleep. Of course her dark brown hair was all messed up, and most of her makeup was gone, but she still radiated with beauty. No matter how much she disputed that, Akira still admired her like a goddess.

Her appearance wasn't all there was to her either, her personality was just as dynamic and unique as her looks. She was into superheroes kind of like Akira, but the movie portrayals more so than their origins in comic books. But that didn't stop her from being interested in knowledge that only a comic book fanatic could reveal. Amy had a distinct sense of humor. She was attractively shy at times, but just the right amount for Akira. She was courteous to his mom and social with friends he would introduce her to. She put effort into every word she said or texted and Akira easily considered her the most intelligent of the women he was ever with, although perhaps, that was just their difference in age. Most importantly, Akira felt like he could never get bored of her company or her conversations. He didn't just feel this, he knew it to be true.

Amy was everything Akira could have possibly wanted in a partner, and more. When he was sick one night, she drove by just to give him a hug and some soup. When he was bored at his friend's house and his friends were all asleep, she watched the same movie as him at the same time on Netflix while they communicated through text message. Akira was happy. Amy seemed happy.

• • •

FEBRUARY 9ᵀᴴ

Akira soon obtained a job with Jake, delivering pizza for the local pizza place named "Anthony's Pizza". He enjoyed his job. He didn't need to dress to meet any standards and he could listen to music all he wanted. Plus, he got to work with his best friend's brother!

"Yeah dude, their entire house REEKED of pot. If I didn't know any better, you'd think I just delivered to Cody himself hahah," Jake laughed through Akira's Bluetooth in his car.

"Well," Jake said, "I'm glad you're digging the job man, sometimes the first week can be tough not knowing streets too well, but then again I guess I underestimated your ridiculous memory again." Akira nodded despite being alone in his car. He was eager to get off work and spend the money he made.

"Wellp, I'll talk to you later dude. Thanks again for the hook up."

Akira got out of his car, and stumbled back into his job and asked Anthony himself if there were any deliveries left. Anthony nodded, and picked one out of the back, put it in a bag and placed it atop the counter. "AY, last one for the night kiddo. Take this, and get yo'self home." Akira did his best to hide his eager smile.

Akira carried the two boxes of pizza and a two liter Pepsi bottle into his car. He arrived at the house with little difficulty since the sun was still shining.

knock knock knock *DING DONG*

Akira stepped back and waited. The older man answered the door right away with a peculiar look on his face. "Ehh, I didn't or-der no Chinese food!" But mid-sentence his smile leaked out, this let Akira know he meant it as a joke. Akira thought it was kind of funny.. the first time he heard it. Now it was the third time some-one referenced his ethnicity in only two days of work.

"Ha....ha....ha, yeah they sent me here to throw you off." Akira did his best to form a convincing smile. He received the payment and a two-dollar tip and began heading to the other side of town. He made out alright for a Thursday night. He pur-chased some flowers from a local supermarket and arrived at Amy's house. The sun was just beginning to set, giving off an orange gleam.

He began walking to her front door while texting her to warn her of his arrival. Akira was nervous about her peering out a win-dow and seeing the flowers in his arm before he wanted, so he made sure to get to the front door before she had a chance.

Although he met and talked with Amy's mom, dad, and sis-ter before, he was still nervous that they'd open the door. He was prone to this type of embarrassment. As the door slid open, Akira realized it was Amy and her younger sister Natalie. Natalie was thirteen years old.

"AWWWWWWW that's so romantic!!!" Natalie shouted while Amy grabbed her head pushed her aside.

"Aw, thank you so much Akira! I'm going to put them in a vase in the kitchen real quick." She kissed him on the cheek then darted back towards the kitchen to place the flowers in a vase. When she came back he was still blushing. He took her hand in his. Then she led him to his car. When they entered the false privacy of the car they hugged and kissed.

I want a boyfriend like that someday... Not Asian though. Just spontaneous and romantic! Natalie sighed and went back upstairs to the safety of her bed and the Disney channel.

Akira took Amy out to eat at a local Applebee's.

Akira enjoyed the food almost as much as getting to know his girlfriend. He suspected she felt the same. Akira admired her all the more for it. After a hot meal and a delicious shared dessert, they went back to a clearing. Akira showed Amy this spot once before, but this time he came prepared. When they parked their car, he took out a backpack. "What's that for?"

"You'll see. Maybe I'm gonna chop you up and put you in here when I'm done.."

"Well, can you at least turn me into a pizza topping for people I don't like?"

"If you're lucky!" They walked through a thick trail surrounded by thick brush on both sides. Atop a hill of sand, he opened the backpack. The hill of sand seemed so out of place. At the top of the hill you could see a major road filled with life.

Street lights, headlights, horns and engines all buzzed blurred. But above that and the tree line, was nothing but outer space. And a damned good view of it too. There was no better spot in all of New York to watch the stars. Or at least that's what they had agreed upon. As Amy got lost in the cosmos, Akira pulled out a blanket from his backpack. He laid it down. When Amy turned around she let out a laugh. The laugh was smothered in approval.

They agreed they both shared a deep passion for a singer named Anthony Green. It was one of the first things in common they discovered when they met. Akira thought he might have to thank Mr. Green one day since that might have been part of the conversation they had prior to their first kiss. Akira took out a speaker from his backpack and started playing Anthony Green's discography.

The transition from conversation to lips colliding was breathtaking. There was no one within a mile radius of the two, and anyone else was unaware of the secluded location. Akira bit her lower lip, and subsequently reached up the back of her shirt. He unhooked her bra while she began to unzip his pants. He thought of how it was finally happening. He knew tonight was the night. Akira wasn't a virgin and he was sure she wasn't either. But he was still filled with feelings of excitement and nervousness. Moments later all that remained was their socks. Luckily Akira brought a second blanket for them. The weather was in the high forties but they didn't care. Twenty minutes and multiple positions later they laid there in each other's warmth, ignoring their discarded clothes. *Wow* was all that went through Akira's mind during the silence, but he felt too nerdy to say it to her. Then he turned over and began kissing her neck. "Wow." Amy said delightfully. Akira pulled back, "Wh-whaat??"

"You, silly!" They continued doing what they were doing. The beauty in what they were doing was reflected off of the candles of the night above. Akira privately wondered if the stars enjoyed watching him instead of the other way around for a change.

On the drive home, Akira didn't notice, but he was driving slowly to savor every minute before dropping Amy off. He felt clingy at times, but he treasured every second he spent. They arrived at her house and she kissed him goodbye. He watched her go to the door and already missed her.

Akira was smiling like an idiot the entire night. He was too happy to fall asleep, if that was even possible. His room seemed vacant of darkness, even with the lights off. He was contemplating texting Cody to inform him of his victory but decided against it. He didn't want to spoil his life's triumph with braggery. A nerd and a goddess. He reimagined the night over and over again in his head until he finally dozed off into sleep.

APRIL 13ᵀᴴ

"HOW DID WE END UP like this?"

"I don't know. I guess nothing good can last forever.." Akira said as he let out a long sigh. He was staring past Amy. He kept visually fixating on a tree being blown side to side outside. It looked like it could have gotten ripped out of the ground at a moment's notice.

"Listen, I don't want to fight. It's been so dumb. We just fight over stupid stuff." Amy was looking down at her plate and moving her food around with her fork as she spoke.

"I agree. Let's just forget about it for now. I'll take you to a movie or we can go bowling!"

"Sure thing." Amy forced a smile and they called the waiter over for the check. He had only been with Amy for a handful of months, but he already knew deep down that he loved her. Despite this, he didn't want to use it as a crutch to work things out. He wanted to work things out with Amy the right way.

• • •

"I dunno dude, she thought I was trying to be sneaky or something.."

"Just cause your phone didn't have service in my house?"

Akira nodded and thought about if there was anything that he did to make Amy distrust him. Cody chimed in abruptly interrupting his thought process.

"Relationships suck dude! I told you, you could of had the same amount of fun without dating her."

Well it's too late for that now, Akira thought, but he remained silent. "I still regret some of the stuff I said in those fights. It stinks. You fight over stupid stuff, and then end up saying even stupider stuff. And we've barely been together more than three months. But after every fight, I feel like we're stronger now that we've pulled together." Cody simply shrugged.

"Jake would probably know better than me. But I feel like him and Angela don't fight that often."

They were hanging out in Jake's basement, only scarcely illuminated by a television. The weather was as cold as ever. It felt more like Winter never left than it did Spring.

Then without warning, Akira's phone started convulsing and fell off of the table. Akira managed to grab it before it hit the floor. The iPhone 8 was an expensive model despite being over a year old. Akira did not recognize the number. He reluctantly brought it up to his ear. In a fraction of a second, he decided he'd let the caller speak first. This way he could guess what kind of call he was answering, and if it was worth his time.

"Hello.. is this Akira Kishimoto?"

"This is he, who is this?"

The female voice hesitated for a moment. Akira didn't pick up on it. Instead he was trying to figure out who this person was.

"My name is Christine.. I work over at Stony Brook Hospital.. I'm afraid I have some bad news. Your mother was transported here via ambulance earlier today."

Akira immediately wanted to ask if she was alright. He didn't know what could have happened and barely managed to hold the phone to his head. He remained silent, waiting and listening.

"She's alright. She fainted at her job and we're just running diagnostic scans on her to make sure everything's alright."

"Thank God."

"Yes, she's very sorry to worry you but we needed to call someone to notify them and you're the only emergency contact that's family."

"Oh.. I see. So when will she be released?"

"It shouldn't be too long now. She'll call you when she can. It will probably be later tonight." Akira was unconsciously frowning.

He told the lady thanks and hung up.

"Is everything alright?" Cody was genuinely concerned. Akira lifted the phone from his cheek. His arm then dropped as if it were going limp. Cody thought he was going to drop the phone too. Then he noticed Akira was gripping it very tightly.

"My mom's in the hospital." He let out at last. Saying it made Akira feel even worse. It made it that much more real.

"Dude.." Cody looked tense. He seemed like he was struggling for the right words. "I'm so sorry. If you need anything let me know man. I hope she's alright man." Cody tended to overuse words like "man" and "dude" when he was shocked.

Akira forced a smile. His whole world shook. Then it became more of a vibration. Then he realized it was actually his silenced phone back in his pocket. He took it out hoping it was his mom. It was Amy. Akira looked at the phone harshly, then slowly put it back in his pocket. He didn't want to deal with anything other than his hospitalized mother at that moment. He didn't know how he'd be able to tell Amy what was going on either. Or maybe he just didn't want to. *It'll be okay. It'll be okay. It'll be okay. It'll be-*

• • •

"Your call has been forwarded to an automated voice messaging system. 6-3-1-5-5-5-1-8-9-4 is not available. At the tone please record your message. When you finish recording you may hang up or press one for more options."

Amy opted to hang up. She wasn't a big fan of voicemails. She never was. Although she remembered one that Akira left her a month ago. He rambled on for almost ten minutes about how much he missed her cute face. She listened to it several times before she deleted it after their first bad fight. Flashing back to the present, Amy sat there wondering why Akira didn't speak to her all day. Why didn't he answer his phone? *That oriental bastard is always on his phone,* she mused. She wanted things to work out, she really did.

Her home life wasn't too great. Amy nearly got into a fist fight with her dad that week. Tensions were up like fireworks because she told her dad her mom was "Stupid to stay with his cheating ass." It wouldn't be the first time he hit her. That was years ago though..now, Amy was twenty-one. She wanted to move out. She wanted to get away. She wanted more than Akira could currently give. That last thought was quickly swept under her mental blanket, so it could be reviewed later. Amy yawned. She'll talk to him tomorrow. It'll be a new day. More energy to deal with everything. She stripped to her underwear and bra and went to sleep early.

$$\cdot \; \cdot \; \cdot$$

APRIL 18TH

Steam flooded the bathroom as hot water pounded away at Akira's worries. He was convincing himself things would be alright. He knew they would be. That's how life worked right? Then all of sudden his phone with it's volume turned on to the max, roared. Akira jumped out of the shower barely shutting it off on his way out. The warm water he was drenched in became colder and colder as Akira ran to his phone. Steam filed out of the bathroom after him. He didn't bother dressing, only making sure his hands were dry. He answered the call he was waiting for.

"Hey hun! I'm really sorry to scare you like that."

"No it's perfectly alright Mom. It's just been a while since I've had a scare like that, so I was worried. Do they know why you fainted?"

Water from Akira's long dark bangs were beginning to drip on his phone.

"They're not really sure.. It was a normal day in class. Then I remember walking out of the classroom. I don't know why, but then I went to the teachers' lounge."

Lin sounded as uncertain as she felt. She had no recollection of anything after leaving her classroom. "My co-worker Mr. Matthews said he saw me just drop out of nowhere. He tried waking me up, and even splashing water in my face. When that didn't work they called an ambulance. The next thing I knew; I was in the ER."

Akira swallowed. "So..when are you going to be coming home?"

Lin elegantly brushed off his question. Her voice was always disarming even when she scolded Akira. "Did you eat supper yet?"

"Yeah, at the Johnsons'."

"Excellent. I should be home making breakfast before you know it. Get some rest Akira. I love you."

"I love you too mom. I will." But he didn't. He didn't fall asleep until 3 AM. Akira was plagued by the very notion of anything being wrong with his mother. She was the most important person in the world to him. He finally ended up tearing up at the thought. That's when he decided he had enough worrying because she was going to be fine. This was the third time his mind came to that conclusion that day. Akira forced himself to think of other things until he finally dozed off.

• • •

APRIL 22ND

"Another Long Island Iced Tea please."

Amy tipped the bartender and walked back to her hotel room. Her and a few friends went on vacation to Ocean City, Maryland. She wasn't sure she was even herself anymore. It seemed like her first year of college in Cortland all over again. Back then she was in an abusive relationship. Her boyfriend didn't trust her, so he treated her like shit. Finally, she broke down. After over a year of belittlement, she transcended her morals to fulfill his prophecy. She cheated on her boyfriend. Eventually their relationship ended, just as all things do. But when one of her friend's friends tried to kiss her and she didn't push back right away, she felt way guiltier.

They were just enjoying a deep conversation. Then all of their friends left the room, and before she knew it he came in for the kiss. After a moment, or two, she pushed him away. She said she had a boyfriend. "I understand," he said compassionately. But he hung around her all of that night. The next day he began texting her. Amy didn't want to ignore him, but she didn't want to answer either. She didn't want to hurt Akira, especially knowing that his mother was in and out of the hospital for the past week and a half. He drove her all the way to her friend's house that they all departed from. He had brought her flowers again and he finally opened up about what was wrong with him. He did so apologetically, and it crushed her.

This new boy, Jack, just happened to know one of her friends they went to Ocean City with. Since then every night him and his friends insisted in meeting up. Amy enjoyed her escape from her life, but just like the crazy party nights at Cortland, she eventually just wanted it to end. On the way back she texted Jack back with as little excitement or interest as she could feign. She wavered whether or not she would tell Akira of her screw up. She told the friend she trusted most on the trip. Alice suggested that it wasn't important because of all the things going on with his mom. Amy didn't know if she agreed because of logical reasons, or emotional reasons. And that scared her the most.

• • •

MAY 1ST

The toughest part of the day wasn't school. It didn't matter if it was tests, projects, group assignments or extra loads of homework. In fact, Akira welcomed the distractions. No, it was work that was the hardest. Akira just couldn't get used to faking smiles every time he went on a delivery. He wished he could acquire a mask and wear it without judgement. He wanted to quit his job so bad sometimes. He really didn't want to interact with anyone more than he had to, let alone smile with a prevarication that burned a hole in his brain.

Cody and Jake always asked him to hang out, have a couple of beers, chill and play video games, or get some food. He politely denied all of their attempts. He managed to see Amy a few times since his mother was hospitalized. He didn't know how to talk to her any more than he already had about what was going on. She only knew the surface. She was acting differently too, although he couldn't tell if it was because she was unsure of how to comfort him or something else.

It has been a week since Akira's mom became comatose. The doctors still didn't know why. They were essentially useless to Akira. Overpaid messengers of bad news.

He went to visit once and it made him nauseous. He couldn't bare it when she didn't respond to his conversation. He left almost immediately after. He didn't even say goodbye. Not that it mattered. Could she even hear him? Understand him? These questions burned through Akira's brain like a forest fire. He avoided visiting her since that day. An entire week of insufferable loneliness at home. It was so eerily quiet that he left music players on 24/7. Sometimes it'd be the TV instead. Occasionally, both. He just didn't want to come home to the painful silence. With silence, Akira couldn't ignore his mother's absence. Sometimes he muttered things to himself to hear his own voice reverberate within the empty walls of his apartment.

Finally, on another cold night where Akira's closest companion was a six pack of beer, he got a text he was half-expecting.

"Listen Akira. I just don't think I'm at a point in my life where I want a boyfriend. I can't give you all that I am. You know a little bit about my bad home life, but it's way worse than I could ever explain. I'm so sorry that I can't help you more while your mother is away. I don't want things to be bad between us because I care about you, but we need some time apart. *Maybe* in the future something will happen, but for now we have too much going on in our lives."

Akira had never been broken up with in person. This age of technology made him sick sometimes. He felt it was so impersonal. He'd rather talk face to face, but his past girlfriends all took the easy way out. He thought they were selfish. Too guilty to accept that they were hurting him, too weak. Akira didn't really know what to respond back with. So he didn't write back. He was extremely sad, but he cried so much in the past two weeks it was like another day for him. Later that night Cody noticed his relationship change on Facebook. He Facebooked Akira hoping to get an answer out of him. Akira didn't respond to that either. When he thought about it the next morning *it* did hit him and made him weep once more.

• • •

MAY 6TH

Akira left work early driving far faster than he ever had while delivering. He had received a phone call from the intensive care unit informing him that his mom had awoken from the coma. He felt a sudden tidal wave of guilt for not visiting for two weeks straight. He was nervous, sweaty and excited as if he was on a first date. He avoided asking any other questions over the phone.

Akira pulled into a guest parking spot and locked up his car. He went to the information desk. There was a security guard named Jim sitting there.

"Hi, I'd like Lin Kishimoto's room number to visit please."

"Sure thing kid."

Jim pulled out a visitor pass and stuck it on Akira's upper right breast.

"You'll be looking for 438 on the 4th floor. If you get lost just ask someone behind the circular desk."

Akira marched triumphantly up to the elevator, with only a touch of shame in the back of his mind. He pushed the button **4FL**. He braced himself to see the mother who raised him by herself for most of his life in a weakened state. He was happy to know that she was actually good enough to converse with him. Although,

Akira was a bit worried that she didn't call him herself. The elevator doors opened and as Akira was prepared to speed walk out, a nurse pushing a man in a wheelchair impeded his progress. He let them get in before he made another attempt to leave.

Almost in a jog, he watched the numbered doors fall behind him. Some doors were open making it difficult to see the number. Akira saw an unhappy looking patient sitting in front of a TV. Another room was filled with yelling. Some patients had solemn looking family accompanying them. Most had none at all. Akira finally made it to a closed door with **438** on it. He stood there for a moment bracing himself. He was preparing himself mentally when an ear shattering cough erupted from room **439** next to him. He flinched for an instant, calmed himself, then he opened the door and marched right in.

CHAPTER 4

LIN WAS SPEAKING TO A doctor when they both turned and faced Akira who entered slowly. The hospital room was pretty plain. Just like all of the white scrubs the doctors wore. The rooms were as interchangeable as the nurses and doctors that inhabited them.

Akira wondered if they remembered patient's names after they were released or pronounced deceased. Did they even remember their patient's names when they walked out of their respective rooms? He took his cynicism and put it in a box and buried it deep in his mind. This was a time for celebration. His mom was awake and speaking.

"Oh is this your boy?" The doctor asked, smiling.

"Yes. His name is Akira." Lin answered proudly.

"Nice to meet you. We can finish the questions later. I got mostly what we needed for now. Plus, you know how long these blood tests take and what not. I'll see you later Ms. Kishimoto." He nodded towards Akira.

"Thank you Dr. Hockstatter. I appreciate it."

Akira walked over to the bed where his mother was. He felt more like he hovered over towards her. He didn't hear or recognize any of his own footsteps. His gaze was acutely fixed on his mother's face until he began checking out the equipment around her to try to gain insight on anything that was going on. Akira's simple, yet deep thoughts were sharply interrupted.

"It's been too long Akira. I've missed you every second I've been awake. I hope everything has been alright at home. I'm truly sorry that I haven't been there."

"Mom! Please. Don't. You don't hafta apologize for anything. I'm just glad you're doing okay."

Lin's face contorted and for a brief second sadness flickered across her face. When Akira looked back up at her face it flashed back into a heartwarming smile with peaceful but worried eyes.

"They told me I've been out for almost two weeks.."

"The Johnsons' had me over for dinner a few nights, or sometimes Cody or Jake brought it to our apartment. You don't need to worry about me ma."

"That's great! Good people those Johnsons are. I'll have to bake something for Betty one day. How has Amy been?"

"She's been good." Akira lied. He didn't see a point in worrying her over him any more than she already was. Even if the mention of Amy's name made him flinch.

They talked for an hour but Lin became increasingly tired looking.

"Listen Mom, I should get going. I've got work and school tomorrow."

"Sure thing. It's just as well too. I've only been awake for a few hours and I've had to submit to non-stop testing and questioning. They'll resume after visiting hours, so my plan is to get some more rest in before they notice you're gone." She chuckled a little bit and Akira smiled.

"You know what? Maybe I..maybe I should stay here with you.. I can miss schoo-"

"No. It's okay. I'll come home tomorrow and you can see me after work. Don't worry about it." She let out a yawn. Akira hugged her tightly and she put her arms around him. One hand began massaging the back of his head through his hair.

"Listen closely Akira. Life is and always will be about how you perceive it. You alone have the power to control what goes on and how you feel about it," she whispered in an almost secretive, conspiratorial voice.

"Um. Sure thing Mom.."

"Reality is precisely what you make it out to be. And one more thing. You may not realize it yet, but life is also a constant battle between good and evil. There will always be choices, and there will always be decisions. I know my son will make the right ones." They separated from each other slowly.

"Thanks mom. I'll, uh, try my best to keep that in mind. I love you so much.. but I guess I'll see you tomorrow right?"

Lin had already receded back into her hospital bed with her eyes half closed.

"See...you..tomorrow... love you....Akir.." The rest of her sentence was completed with a yawn.

Akira proceeded to leave the room as quietly as possible. This time he did not hear the noise from his steps because he didn't make any.

He was completely puzzled as to what his mother meant. But he eventually decided it was just hospital meds messing with her. Good and evil? Were there movies playing in the background when she was comatose? Akira saw a TV in the room, even though it was off. Akira thought about it the whole way home. Only one more lonely night in the apartment. He was happy. And then he remembered Amy. He remembered how much he missed her. How beautiful she was. How much her touch meant to him. How he treasured her words. How he didn't even get to say goodbye. He broke down and cried since he could finally grieve the demise of his most painful break up.

"Maybe I'll try to get in touch with her tomorrow. Maybe we can work things out." He said to himself. Akira decided that he had gotten all too used to talking to himself out loud at home. He chose to end his one-sided conversation early and go to bed. Lying there he expected to fall asleep a lot easier because of the relief of seeing his mom. But instead, he attempted to decipher his mother's cryptic drug riddled warning/advice. For reasons he couldn't understand, it left him feeling extremely uneasy. He lied dormant in bed until 4 AM. His eyes remained open staring at either the ceiling or one of the adjacent walls. When he finally closed them he began to drift into slumber.

CHAPTER 5

MAY 12^(TH)

AKIRA WAS LOOKING OUTSIDE THE drenched window. It was one of the first rainstorms of the spring season. April showers bring May flowers. But what about when you don't give a damn about flowers anymore? He watched as the rain droplets hit the windshield of the car and stretched out, then elongated around the sides. Akira was fascinated by the ways that Newton's laws took effect.

"Man that's so messed up that she has a boyfriend already. I'm pissed at her." Shot Angela who had a tendency to speak impulsively.

"Ang!!" Jake warned. He figured his friend didn't want to start thinking of his ex-girlfriend and first love so soon after his mother's awakening.

"It's okay. I don't really care that much," lied Akira, "Besides, I have a strong feeling he'll dick her over in no-time."

Cody joined in "Yeah, I mean a guy who drives a Mustang that fast has got to be lacking somewhere."

They'll probably tell me he steals candy from senior citizens next to try to cheer me up.. Akira pondered. Jake and Angela were dropping Akira and Cody off at home from school. They finally arrived and pulled in front of his apartment.

"I guess my mom still isn't home."

"Bro. Do you want us to wait?" Cody suggested.

"No of course not. She'll be home soon anyway. The last time I went they assured me today was the day. I'll talk to you guys tomorrow. Thanks for the ride." Thunder boomed overhead. It masked the sound of Akira shutting the car door.

Akira entered his apartment. He was hungry. But he also didn't want to pester his friends to stop at a food place on the way back. Besides, he wanted to get home as early as he could to clean up the mess he made in the apartment over the last three weeks. Akira took out left overs from a diner. He took the burger out and put it in the microwave. He started cleaning while it was cooking. He put on some doom metal that Jake gave him so he could listen to it out loud without bothering his mom one last time.

He kept his phone beside him incase his mom called.

"...What's that smell..?"

"................"

Then he noticed greyish white smoke coming from the kitchen. "Oh shit!" He yelled as he grabbed a dish towel and wet it in the sink. He saw through the microwave screen that his meal had burst into small flames that were still sparking in short bursts of light. Akira punched the open button and threw the wet towel onto the burger. The wet towel suffocated the flames. They went out quickly. Akira took the spinning microwave platform out. He observed his mess. It smelled awful.

"Pft. Tinfoil. And to think I used to be an honor student." He opened the windows in the apartment before the ancient fire alarm went off. After throwing out his crisp meal the phone rang.

Akira picked it up even though the number was blocked.

"Hello Akira.."

It took almost a moment, but then Akira remembered the only person he knew who uses a blocked number.

"..Why? Why are you bothering me?"

The voice seemed uncertain and unfamiliar. But it was still a voice Akira recognized and never wanted to hear again.

"I don't know how to tell you this.. but your mother, Lin.." The voice trembled a bit. "She passed away this morning."

Akira let out a gasp. It couldn't be true. He was lying. Right? Akira didn't know what to say while he choked on unreality. He wanted to scream. He wanted to deny the very possibility of it being true.

"I'm so sorry." The man said in response to Akira's silence. Tears were already streaming.

Akira wanted to ask how. He wanted to ask why. He wanted to call his father a lying bastard. He wanted his mom to put her key in the door knob and twist it open and surprise him. He wanted to put a knife in his chest and twist it open.

"I'm sorry I can't be there for you my son. I'll wire some money into your checking account but that's the best I can do right now."

Akira was hardly even listening. He was standing in the middle of the kitchen with the phone to his face. In the background of the phone call there was nothing but the burnt smell of tin foil and the droning of extended guitar riffs in loop.

"There's some things you ought to know Akira. Come see me when you're ready. Take your time. You'll figure out how to contact me when you're ready. I loved your mother until the end and I love you both so much."

Liar Akira mouthed the word out. Then his dad hung up. Just like that he was gone. Just as Akira has always known him to be for the last twelve years. Akira dropped to his knees and began crying on the kitchen floor. The tears wet his shirt. They formed a small puddle on the floor beneath him. Cleaning the apartment didn't matter anymore. Nothing did.

PART II
THE DISCOVERY

. . .

CHAPTER 6

MAY 24ᵀᴴ

"DID YOU HEAR HIS MOM passed away?" Alice asked with a sorrowful inflection that pricked Amy's heart.

"Yeah," *Don't remind me.* She thought. "It's so sad. I honestly didn't even think something like that could have happened."

"Then again I guess neither of us knew anyone in a coma before that."

"Is it true that he moved in with Cody and Jake?" Amy wondered out loud.

"You should know! You're friends with Angela."

"Not really anymore. Ever since me and Akira broke up things have been weird."

There was a knock on the door and Amy's sister opened it in the distance.

"Jack's here!!" she called out.

"Hey wassup babe. Sup Alice."

"Hi Jack." They both said simultaneously.

"Did you guys just see a ghost or something? You both look so goddamn sad that you're depressing me." He walked over and put his arm around Amy and kissed her.

"It's nothing babe, don't worry about it." Amy smiled and put all the thoughts of her past behind her. She had her own things to worry about like going apartment hunting with Alice and Jack so she can get away from her stupid family. She did feel kind of bad about leaving her sister, but they treated her like an innocent princess most of the time anyway.

She didn't go to Akira's mom's funeral. But then again, would going have made it worse for him?

"Come on out and see the Mustang Amy, I got it lookin' as fine as you now!"

She gave him a distracted smile and went to him.

• • •

Akira lived in a guest room in the basement of the Johnson's house. The basement was complete with a bathroom, a small kitchen, a shared closet and two bedrooms. The guest room which Akira occupied was still filled with his boxes of unpacked possessions. The room adjacent was Jake's. When he wasn't making love to Angela he was usually smoking weed. Akira joined him when he did the latter.

The former tended to be loud and awkward. Thank God for headphones!

He knew it wasn't great to rely on an escape such as pot. But he didn't view it as something he needed to make it through the day. Instead, Akira felt like it simply made him able to take slightly more joy in things like video games, TV shows and of course food. Taking more joy in those things means being less depressed. Akira reasoned that if smoking weed was an escape, then what the fuck were anti-suppressants supposed to be, candy?

Akira's grades dropped steadily at first. Then it was as if they jumped off a cliff. If it weren't for the interference of a guidance counselor informing his teachers, Akira would have failed out by this point. Only three weeks of school were left before graduation.

Akira had heard from Amy twice since they broke up when she would virtually check up on him via text message. He didn't ask if she were still dating *Jack, who beats up senior citizens for candy. Jack who is probably that asshole you hate on the freeway with the nicer car and the beautiful girl riding shotgun cutting everyone off.* Instead, they talked about how things were at his new residence and the occasional "I hope you're doing alright". *I'd be better if you came over and gave me a reason to want to be alive* he had thought and not said. What's done was done. If Akira didn't learn this in the last month, then he had learned nothing.

Whenever he had time, he would go to the studio that Cody and Jake's band rented out. Jake had been teaching him how to play drums for a little over a year. He wasn't that good, but banging on the drums was the best ventilation for his frustration and sadness that he could find. Sometimes he'd scream random words or sentences that could be related to his Mom or Amy. His throat would hurt after, and his thighs and forearms would ache, but he'd feel more calm after. One day he aspired to play drums in a progressive metal band with jazz in it. Maybe one day he'd be good enough for that.

• • •

MAY 28*TH*

"You SUCK at rolling dude." Stated Cooper matter-of-factly. Wu-Tang Clan was blasting in the background of the packed Nissan Sentra. There were multiple conversations taking place. Suddenly, Jake procured his belongings and cleared his throat. "Well guys, I don't feel like waiting a million years for another mediocre joint so me and Angela are gonna go to the bonfire now. See you there."

They got out together and walked a few meters to the beach filled with hyperactive drunk teenagers as well as the all-too-calm stoners. There were three bonfires raging across the beachfront. After Cooper, Cody and Akira finished smoking, they began their search for Jake and Angela. Or anyone else they knew at this multi-high school party. "Wow. it's so weird to see so many different kinds of people here," observed Cody. "It almost makes you wanna... GET MORE DRUNK!" He ran off to get some beers.

"Shit the jocks are here too." Cooper said. Akira's memory flashed back to the multiple incursions Cooper Mills has had with jocks throughout high school. Cooper was a nice guy with a temper. Akira typically only saw him when parties were happening. Akira recalled that he was kicked off of the lacrosse team for getting in a fist fight with someone. Akira's memory sorted through information until he remembered the name Ian McKinley who graduated the year prior. Then Akira remembered Coop got into another fight with Ian after Coop beat up Ian's friend Brent Armstrong for making moves on his girlfriend at the time. Brent also spread rumors when she denied him. That's three fights and Akira was pretty sure he could recall another one, but his flashback was cut short by a tug on his arm from Cooper.

"Yo, why is Tyler Walker and his cronies coming this way?" Akira watched Cooper tense up like he was preparing to fight again. Tyler Walker, Brent Armstrong and two other kids Akira didn't recognize waltzed up to them. They shot Cooper a quick glance and then looked down. Tyler spoke up first.

"Sup Akira. We just wanted to say we heard what happened to your mom. Our condolences." While Cooper's face was filled with disorientation and disbelief Akira's was blank.

"Fuck you." Akira said after moment's pause. Tyler's face was astonished while Brent's showcased rage.

"What did you just say?" Brent spat. Tyler frowned. "We were just trying to be nice, what the hell man?" Cooper looked worriedly at Akira. His face was still blank.

"I said 'fuck you guys'. You called me and my best friend faggots not even a month ago. You made fun of me throughout middle and high school and bullied me in like every single gym class. Then you come over here with the 'It's senior year and we're all friends' facade? Just to ease your own conscience? No, go fuck yourself."

Cooper's jaw dropped. Brent's face reddened like a red balloon and Tyler's frown turned into a look of contempt. "I'd kick your ass right now if you weren't an orphan." Brent shot. Tyler glanced at Cooper. "Naw. These pussies aren't worth it. We were just being polite. You ever say anything like that again and you're dead kid. We'll make you and your faggot friends cry." They turned their backs and went over to the biggest of the three bonfires.

Cody walked over and handed them beers. "What the hell just happened!? What did you do Cooper?"

"It actually wasn't me dude!"

Akira who had already finished the beer he was given, crushed it in his hand. "Wow what a rush. I told those guys how it was. They were only being sympathetic because the girls they're trying to get with were watching." Cody who was very good at avoiding conflicts because he didn't care what anyone thought of him was impressed. "Cheers to the new Akira I guess."

He tossed Akira another brew and they chugged together. Then they stumbled over to the smallest of the bonfires.

Cooper told the less popular kids around the fire about what Akira did. Many of these kids were bullied by that friend group in the past and were laughing out loud and cheering. These kids were sick of being called 'losers', 'fags', 'gays' and whatever other intelligently crafted insults could be created and thrown at them by the jocks. By the end of the night everyone at the bonfire had heard of what happened. Then one of the freshman named Pat who was friends with multiple groups of people walked over to Tyler and Brent and asked them why there were afraid to fight Cooper and Akira.

"Why on God's green Earth would we be afraid of that frail chink and his idiot friend?" Brent was pissed off and every word he said showed it. Then Ian McKinley was behind him. He had just arrived. "You're *afraid* of *those* nerds?" He laughed hoarsely. "I didn't take you for a chump Brent. But maybe what Miranda said was true. You've got no dick." Ian sneered and watched Cody trail off down the beach towards a big rock.

"You find their car. I'll teach the wimpy one a lesson." Ian, who was also bullied throughout middle school and early high school until he started working out religiously, took pride in being empowered. He's been a proud bully ever since. He walked over to the big rock a few feet away. Cody Johnson zipped up his zipper after urinating and turned around straight into a punch in the face.

Brent took out a switchblade and began releasing the air out of the tires of a Nissan Sentra. "I don't know about this man; this seems a little extreme. To be honest, I'd rather just kick the shit out of them." Tyler said, then let out a nervous laugh. Brent gave him a disappointed look.

"Too late. Three flat tires. Those assholes can suck on that." Although referring to Cooper and Akira, Brent was also thinking about the time he made out with Miranda Loshner while she was dating Cooper at a party. She was wasted but she *suddenly* remembered she had a boyfriend and walked home. When she stopped answering his texts, Brent sent her a picture of his penis. This picture would be seen by her entire friend group by the end of the week.

As they drove away from the bonfire they passed a police officer. No doubt going to break up the party. "Tonight's our lucky night!" Joe Fonte said from the backseat glancing over at the cop car.

"COPS!!!!" Shouted an indistinguishable voice. People began scattering and panicking. "I can't get anything else on my record or I'll be screwed, get the brothers and let's go!" Cooper said while debating if getting rid of his bowl was worth it or not.

"What the hell happened to you?" Jake asked with a bemused look on his face.

"It's not important now, let's just get out of here." Cody replied with a bloody nose and swollen eye. The cop's sirens and blinding light was now visible throughout the entire beach. Most people knew alternate escape routes. Akira saw Angela first and thought *Yup her and Jake had sex tonight.* Then he saw a distraught Jake with his arm around his younger brother. Cody held an ashamed and worried look. Without inquiring what happened they hurried to the car. They got in, went in reverse and immediately noticed the deficient tires. Then Cooper's car said: "Warning tire pressure low!"

"Cool, thanks Captain Obvious. SHIT."

The cop was letting people go past him. He wasn't here to arrest anyone, just break up the fun. When he noticed Cooper's car wasn't leaving he walked over and knocked on the window.

"Uh, hello officer! We were just trying to leave but someone slashed our tires!" Cooper said defiantly. The cop looked down at one of the tires.

"That sucks. Get a tow truck. If you're still here in an hour, I'll have to take you guys in for underage drinking. And I swear if I find any marijuana smoking devices you'll regret it." He walked back towards the beach with his flashlight pointed at the nearest teens. Jake felt like using the rage he felt for what happened to Cody to push the car the rest of the way home. They waited forty minutes for a tow truck. During the wait they made fun of the way the police officer called them *marijuana smoking devices*. They wondered out loud if he would call their lighters marijuana incineration devices. Cody did whatever he could to keep any of them from questioning him about his injuries.

• • •

Akira was very ready to sleep when he got "home". He wasn't sure if he could call it that, but the Johnson family did their best to make it feel that way.

Sometimes after playing on his phone he would instinctively go to call his mom and then remember she's not there anymore. At first he even would call anyway just so it could go to voicemail and he could hear her soothing voice. "Hi, you've reached Linda Kishimoto, leave your number and I'll get back to you. Thanks!" Her real name *was* Lin. But when she moved to America from China she adjusted it to Linda. Her close friends still called her Lin regardless. Then, the payments for her cell phone expired and his mother's voice was replaced by a neutral computerized voice. "I guess even that trace of her is gone now.." Akira had said to himself before weeping more one night.

He turned on his side and put the TV on to help him fall asleep. He eventually drifted just as more reality TV rubbish was coming on next.

Akira woke up back at the beach. The three bonfires were ever prevalent. Now their flames danced on the beachfront. Akira was practically memorized by the swirling fire. But all of the faces of the people surrounding the fires were blackened out. Their faces were utterly featureless. Akira felt shivers go up his back as he walked past these husks. Then he noticed the outfit him and Cooper were wearing that same night. He walked over and upon closer inspection noticed the husks wearing his and Cooper's clothes weren't actually moving. None of them were. But the sounds of chatter, laughter, and drunken camaraderie were definitely going on despite the freeze frame image he stared upon. Akira walked over and looked at the indistinguishable face with the dark shading wearing his clothes. He pushed it and it fell backward, but it's arms and legs were in the same position. It was as if it was suffering from rigor mortis. It was very creepy.

Then Akira noticed from his peripheral vision some sand get kicked up from behind a large rock. Something actually moved? Akira started running to this and then his run slowed into a careful stroll. *What if I don't want to see what caused that. Where am I? Is this a nightmare? It has to be. Those faces. That one wearing my clothes...* But his curiosity persisted over the goosebumps he felt. He walked over towards the rock. He began circling it and then as he rounded it, he saw something his mind expected least.

CHAPTER 7

SAND KICKED UP IN FRONT of him as Ian McKinley's foot rotated below him when he launched his leg beneath him. He connected a kick with Cody Johnson's lower stomach. Right in the solar plexus. Then he reached forward and grabbed Cody's arm. He turned and used his own weight to throw Cody forward onto the ground. When Cody was on the ground he spat out some blood--no, Akira realized it was coming from his nose and he was moving to talk. "What the hell is your-" Ian launched a kick into Cody's face which connected with his eye. Sand went up beyond the rock showering Cody's long dirty blonde hair with it.

"HEY YOU DICK!" Akira yelled and ran at Ian. Ian did not look up as Akira went to punch him in his smug face. *I'm gonna regret this later but this douche deserves it* he thought, while forgetting all of the shadowy faces on the other side of the large rock. Akira's fist went straight into Ian's cheekbone...and then came out the other side of his head. Akira had put so much force in the right hook that he lost his balance and fell through Ian landing face first into the ground.

He did not feel the connection of the punch, but he did feel his face collide with the millions of sand particles at once. For a moment he saw nothing but blackness. Then he lifted his face out of the sand and wiped some of it off while turning to look and see how that was physically possible. He turned and Ian and Cody were gone. Then he heard the sound of a zipper and looked three feet to his right only to see Cody with Ian walking up behind him. As Cody began turning, Ian wound up a punch and launched it into Cody's nose while Cody maintained a confused look. He fell back and then caught himself. Cody back stepped twice while clasping his hands to his nose. When he looked up at Ian a kick drilled into his solar plexus knocking his breath away.

"Defend yourself god damnit!" Akira said through his clenched teeth.

Akira got back up and went to swing at Ian again while Ian grabbed Cody's arm from where it was holding his stomach and threw him down. But Akira's hit was once again ignored by Ian's intangible form. That was when Akira realized that he was watching exactly what just happened, happen again. He waited, almost like a movie with a rewind button as they disappeared and reappeared to their "starting positions". *No, it's more like someone keeps hitting the reset button.* Akira just wanted this nightmare to end. Watching his friend get assaulted and not being able to do anything about it was exhausting..

"STOP HURTING MY BEST FRIEND!" He shouted once more in vain. "You can do this Cody!". On the fourth "replay" after their forms flicked back to the beginning of the scuffle, Cody turned around after zipping up his zipper, and Ian threw his punch. But this time Cody ducked under it. Ian looked dazed as Cody charged forward and tackled him. They both landed on the ground. Cody began punching the hell out of Ian's face until Ian rolled. Now Ian was on top and dominating. A few punches to the jaw and Akira looked away.

What could he do? Go back and hang out with the shadow faces at the bonfires? No. He would try helping Cody no matter how futile it was. He walked towards their scuffle, because he decided running might hurt if he phased through them again, and sent a side kick out. For reasons Akira couldn't understand it connected this time. The force of Akira's foot on Ian's face sent him two feet off of Cody. Cody turned and looked up at Akira. "Akira.. you're here…" Before Akira could reply everything went completely dark. It was as if someone simply flicked the light switch off. Before Akira's eyes could adjust to the darkness something hard struck him in the face.

CHAPTER 8

AKIRA WAS SUDDENLY JERKED AWAKE and heard a slight ringing sound. It reminded him of a phenomenon that happens after seeing a really loud concert without ear protection.

His vision returned to him and he adjusted to the light. When he turned, he found Jake staring at him. "Wake up Akira." Akira had a glazed look in his eyes.

"What was that for man?" Akira asked, unsure if he should bring up his weird nightmare. "Cause," he started with a serious coldness in his eyes. "We're going to go to Ian McKinley's house and we are gonna fuck him up."

Akira froze. It was like Jake read his mind, perhaps even knew what he dreamt about. "What time is it?" He wondered out loud.

"I heard Cody talking in his sleep. He was flinching and turning over rapidly. He said..." Jake turned his face in disgust and then continued: "He said 'Fuck you Ian what did you do to Akira?'". Jake looked madder than Akira could ever remember him being. Usually both of the brothers were the epitome of the word 'chill'.

"I think Ian jumped him back at the bonfire. My brother's never been in a fight before. He must have been traumatized. I'll make him pay."

Akira thought things over. It was a lot to handle after an intense dream. Akira was still recalling what happened in the dream and trying to process Jake's fury.

"Oh, and it's 6:30. We've still got time to bash the shit out of his car."

Akira in his exhausted state, was tempted to tell Jake to go do it himself. He avoided this selfish comment and replaced it with a more sensible one. "Jake, an eye for an eye will leave the whole world blind. He'll know it was one of us. What if he goes for Cody again as retribution?" Jake scrunched up his nose. He looked upset. *Smashing the crap out of Ian's car would probably be very therapeutic for him,* Akira thought. Jake let out a frustrated sigh.

"Yeah, but that would also mean I woke you up for nothing." Jake said this with a half-smile still trying to convince Akira, and probably himself too. Akira observed him clench his fist as he thought of his other vengeful options.

"What's going on in here?" Cody asked with innocent curiosity. Akira looked at Cody's blackened eye and remembered his dream from only moments ago. Had he really seen what happened? Was that possible? Or did his subconscious try to piece together what happened while he was asleep? He vividly saw his fist phasing through Ian's cheekbone. The feeling of nothingness was still there which was a direct clash to the feeling of hitting the coarse sand face first.

"Bro.. I know Ian McKinley jumped you last night. And I'm going to kick his ass."

Cody's face transformed into a frown at the mention of Ian's name. But then it became something of a smirk. He was staring intently into his elder brother's eyes.

Then he glanced in Akira's direction.

"You don't need to. I already did."

• • •

48

One day later and Akira was still thinking about everything Cody had said. Cody had told him and Jake about how he had kicked Ian's ass---with the help of Akira in his dream. Cody had told them that it was good enough for him despite Jake's protests. He was just happy his nightmare had ended. In Cody's nightmare he kept reliving the experience. Cody spoke ecstatically about how he couldn't stop reliving Ian's violence. Then he started to hear Akira's voice. Eventually Akira appeared and kicked Ian off of him. Just like the dream Akira had. Akira guessed it wasn't uncommon for best friends to share a dream. But every single detail Cody mentioned was spot on what happened in Akira's version. It was peculiar to say the least. For some reason, Akira didn't feel comfortable telling Cody yet.

A few people in school were gossiping about what happened to Cody's face. He rolled with the punches (so to speak) and told people half-heartedly he got it from fighting off ninjas. Regardless, word had spread that it was Ian McKinley's doing. Which meant that Ian or one of his friends bragged about it and it got out and spread through the social hierarchy.

That pissed Akira off, especially because Ian wasn't even in high school anymore. Coincidentally as he was thinking angry thoughts, Akira overheard someone talking outside at lunch. "... .. Jake Johnson… pussy… Ian…him up..

Akira moved in closer and listened. It was Joe Fonte speaking. Akira couldn't stand Joe because he was an asshole. But he still wasn't Akira's least favorite because Akira felt bad for him. He was a dumb asshole. He followed the others because he didn't know any better.

"If Jake sends him any more threatening messages, we'll kick his ass too." Fonte said from his dumb mouth. Then his dumb mouth opened again when he redirected his dumb words towards Akira. "What you lookin' at Chink-moto?"

Brent Armstrong who was leaning against a wall next to the outdoor jock table walked over.

Akira instantly thought of a T-Rex. Large and dangerous. Small brained and complete with an almost primal tendency towards displaying aggression. *The only thing that separated Brent and a T-Rex is the latter has small arms..*

"You listenin' in on our convo about your pal? No wonder you guys caught us off-guard at Pearl Harbor!" It was times like this where Akira wished he was full Chinese so he could tell Brent he's a racist idiot. He was a racist idiot, but Akira was still half-Japanese too.

"Your friends are all pussies, just like you. Now get out of here herb." When Brent Armstrong first spoke, his words were savage. But by the time he was finished his tone was disinterested. As if Akira wasn't even important enough, or worth his time. Akira, like Cody, was never in a fist fight before. Brent walked up only a few inches away from his face. Akira wasn't afraid of Brent, but he couldn't get his body to stop trembling. There was a pit in his stomach, but Akira still thought that none of this showed on the outside. At least that's what he was hoping for. Akira was putting so much energy into making sure that his intimidation didn't show that he forgot to say something witty. Brent seemed to interpret Akira's silence as resilience. Brent began to display rage again then it disappeared as he backed up. Then without warning he lurched forward again and Akira flinched. A deeply satisfied Brent and his friends all burst out laughing.

Embarrassed and flustered, Akira went back inside the school and sat down by himself. He took out his iPod. It was an old outdated model that wasn't made anymore. He put on music and put his head down. His shame turned into anger at his helplessness. His mom died. His girlfriend broke up with him. He couldn't even back up his words or stand up for his friend. Helplessness might as well have been his middle name.

• • •

The fridge yielded nothing of interest for Akira. It was 2 AM and Akira built up an appetite wasting his life away. He watched an entire television series that night. He returned to his bedroom empty handed. Jake and Angela were out somewhere. He had the entire basement to himself. He turned off the TV and starting playing music. He wished he could beat up Brent and all his friends. Akira's eyes finally closed. His eyeballs began rotating behind his lids like bowling balls. Sleep came over him.

Suddenly Akira was walking in a dark alley way. There were no buildings this big anywhere near where he lived, but Akira wasn't thinking about that. At the end of the alley way was a really bright light. This white light was what captured Akira's attention. As the end of the alleyway transformed into a tunnel, loud cheering began. It made Akira think of wrestlers from the old programs. When they came out into the ring, the fans went crazy to the sound of their theme music. Akira finally exited the tunnel, which led into a gigantic stadium.

METLIFE STADIUM was written in huge lettering on the wall opposite of where Akira entered. There were football players everywhere. Some were throwing passes. Some were practicing tackling dummies. Others were simply jogging or doing pushups. The stadium was packed out. An announcer was yelling enthusiastically. "AND NUMBER 31 BRENT ARMSTRONG THROWS ANOTHER PERFECT PASS. GET READY LADIES AND GENTS, THE GIANTS' VERY OWN MVP IS GOING TO SINGLEHANDEDLY WIN THE NEXT GAME. JUST YOU WAIT!"

Akira turned around quickly as the booming of a Cheerleaders voices came from right behind them. They were all cheering for Brent Armstrong. Akira wasn't an avid football fan, but he could have sworn cheerleaders cheered silently in the major leagues. He noticed with great interest that some of the cheerleaders were familiar. A few were girls from school. Some were famous actresses or even porn stars. Akira took no pleasure in knowing that he could recognize those, but he had to keep his mind off Amy somehow.

"Jesus. I'm having another nightmare. This is ridiculous." Akira didn't know what to do or where to go when suddenly the whole stadium shook.

"WILL YA LOOK AT THAT. THE OPPOSING TEAM JUST ARRIVED. BUT THEY'RE A LITTLE SHORT. THE ONLY MEMBER OF THE DALLAS COWBOYS TO SHOW HIS FACE IS AKIRA KISHIMOTO!" Akira only half-heard this when he realized the practice dummies were replaced with Cooper, Jake and Cody. The football players had no facial features beneath their helmets. They were just like the shadow faces. Except these ones were in motion. They assaulted the now living practice dummies without holding back. Akira's best friends cried out in pain. Cody took a shoulder check that made Akira cringe. They couldn't even defend themselves.

"FUCK YOU BRENT. FUCK YOU! I'M SO SICK OF YOU." Akira shouted at the top of his lungs. The entire stadium went silent. All of the faceless football players stopped what they were doing except for one. One with very noticeable features. Very angry features.

Brent was running directly at Akira. Closing his eyes, Akira said: "I am not afraid. I will not fear you. You will fear me, because I am not a mindless clone like you are. I am my own individual self and I should not be fucked with." He did his best to remain unperturbed. His mind was calm. After all, it was only a dream, *right?*

Even Brent froze at Akira's statement. But something wasn't right. Akira let out his breath. Then disorientation flooded him when he realized that Brent wasn't just stopped, he was frozen mid run. Suddenly, a hole tore through the universe in front of him. The hole was almost a three dimensional orb. An image was focusing inside of it. Akira stepped closer. Everything around him was unchanged, frozen in time. Everything except him and the massive orb-like hole. Akira could feel that it was almost alive. It completely eclipsed Brent Armstrong. But somehow he knew Brent was a statue. Akira stared at this hole and realized it was a portal and felt sweat rush down his face. The image cleared and he couldn't quite believe what he was looking at.

CHAPTER 9

THE AUDIENCE WAS FROZEN MID-CHEER. The commentator's slammed fist remained in a hammer on the table and his other hand was holding his ear piece with the other. Football players were like featureless statues at night. Brent Armstrong was running towards Akira Kishimoto, who was ruining his best dream ever when everything stopped.

There was a loud piercing roar as a Tyrannosaurus Rex began ripping a human apart with its partner. Brent Armstrong was a small toddler on the couch crying. His mom and her boyfriend got up during the movie to go to the bedroom. They figured the movie would keep him occupied long enough for their alone time. He was always bothering her. Sometimes she wished she had more kids just so they could bother each other. Brent stared in horror, unable to turn away. Gore seeped out of the newly separated upper body and lower body. A young boy's terrified curiosity. There was an audible crunch, from which part of the corpse, Brent was unsure, but he was certain of his very terrifying newfound fear. His mom's boyfriend had bought a special Blu-Ray disc that contained all five *Jurassic Park* movies in the series. They played one after another. Brent watched hours of footage, and his mom was only slightly concerned when he ignored the dinner she brought out. "Mommy I'm scared." She patted his head and went back to her boyfriend. When Brent passed out he had his first of many night-mares about the murderous Jurassic Period carnivores.

Akira stared intently into this portal. He didn't know how he knew that Brent only watched four out of five of the movies. Or that his mom loathed his neediness. He didn't know what was go-ing on or...why..his..hands..were glowing...

Akira reached out towards the portal with his blue illuminated hands. Once his fingers were centimeters away, the portal imme-diately collapsed inwards on itself and disappeared. Akira blinked his eyes, and then in that second the portal was back. It came back the size of a small marble, then to the size of a table in a fraction of a second. It was expanding rapidly like someone was pumping air into it. A loud explosion of energy rushed out. Akira found himself again feeling like the entity was alive. It suddenly sent a wave past Akira with a purely red color. The words *blood energy* came to mind in the instant it took to swallow him and the rest of the stadium whole.

As abruptly as the red vortex came, it was gone. The rest of the stadium returned to normal. Brent continued his charge to-wards Akira. Akira stood in disbelief. At this point he knew he was dreaming for certain. He was prepared to let Brent punch him in the face to wake him up. Brent was only a few feet away when his fast charge stopped.

Brent stopped so short he nearly fell forward. Then Kishimoto realized Brent was looking behind him... and above him. Akira dramatically turned around. That was when he slowly began to hear screams and shrieks of terror. In the stands of the MetLife Stadium there were velociraptors chasing after members of the audience. Some had already succumbed to their demises. People hung over the barrier's, arms outstretched. Others were still screaming while they were getting eaten alive by the ferocious raptors. Many members of the audience didn't stand a chance. Other's fell from the upper levels or were pushed off while fleeing. Bodies were dropping onto the stadium like a human waterfall. These victims were already robbed of their faces. But when they died they sounded so human, it was terribly unsettling.

Then more screams. Closer screams.

Brent backed away from Akira in horror. Then he turned to run and saw a T-Rex chasing after members of the football team. One of them, Joe Fonte was hiding behind Cooper. Cooper was still tied down and looked scared. But Joe was nearly crapping himself. Especially once the T-Rex went over to him. It used its height advantage to lean over the training dummy and bite Joe's upper body. His legs kicked and flailed as he got picked up. Then they heard a distinct crunching sound that seemed to echo throughout the stadium and Joe's lower half dropped back to the field. It was still twitching and convulsing. A spine was sticking out like a severed electrical wire. Except instead of sparks of electricity there was spurts of blood. Brent knelt over and puked. It was just like the scene from the movie.

It was the most amazing sight he had ever seen. For some reason, Akira didn't feel as scared as he felt he should have been. Then he heard the fast pitter patter of a Velociraptor charging on the field in his direction. He was telling his legs to run but they wouldn't. "Oh fuck. Oh fuck. Oh fu-" he said, until the Velociraptor literally ran right past him. The speedy apex predator jumped and pounced right onto Brent. Its weight caused him to collapse into his puke face down. He tried to struggle but it's sharp, clawed toes held down on of his legs and one of his arms. Before he could figure out a wrestling move to save himself it bent forward and bit into his jugular vein. Akira heard gurgling noises as everything faded to black.

• • •

It was a boiling hot day. It already felt like 1 PM on a summer day and it was only 10 AM in May. Akira left one of his classes to go to the bathroom. The entire walk consisted of scornful thoughts about how the only air conditioned areas in the school were the office and the library. Then Akira saw Brent stumble in through the main entrance. Brent Armstrong was looking down at his feet. There was something off about him. Akira smirked. The last time he saw Brent, he got his neck ripped out. Now he was coming to school late. Before Akira could realize he was standing in the middle of the hallway like a dimwit, Brent looked up at him. His gaze locked eyes with Akira and then flinched and went back down. They went down as fast as a seesaw when an elephant sits down on one side.

Brent walked into the Alaskan office filled with the privileged leaders of the school to receive his punishment for being late. Akira kept walking towards the bathroom. "What was that about?" he mumbled. When Brent flinched away from eye contact Akira's smirk disappeared. It made him feel very uneasy. He took one last glance at the former shell of what used to be the town's best running back, and then the hallway walls began obstructing his view.

Was Brent like that.. because of me?

Akira's curiosity finally got the best of him. When he got back from school he asked Cody for all the details about the dream they shared. Cody only remembered certain aspects, but everything he recalled happened in Akira's version. *What was the connection? Why is this happening? How is this happening? Why am I sharing dreams with people?* Akira stayed up the entire night writing logical conclusions and looking on the internet for any other cases like his. While searching, he came across a term that sparked his interest. It seemed more relevant than most of the crap Akira was finding. He clicked on a link to LUCID DREAMING and exed out of an ad that popped up saying THERE ARE HORNY SINGLE MOMS IN YOUR AREA!! Akira was reading about how lucid dreaming lets you control your own dreams. Akira felt he could relate to that as of late. Then it began to get less and less useful as more and more articles were wasting his time. 8 FACTS ABOUT LUCID DREAMING. HOW TO BECOME AN EXPERT LUCID DREAMER. HOW TO FUCK THE GIRL OF YOUR DREAMS, IN YOUR DREAMS!

"This is beginning to feel like studying. I hate studying." Akira's patience ran out and he shut the laptop and went to bed. Sifting through the internet is hard enough. Doing it when you're unsure of what you're looking for is even tougher. He was thinking about one of the useful tidbits of information he did pick up. It said lucid dreamers sometimes think about the dream they want to control, before they fall asleep. Akira was pretty sure he was thinking of Brent and Cody on the nights that their dreams intertwined. "Okkkkay Jake good buddy, you're going to be my guinea pig. Let's see if I'm crazy or not." *Then again I'm talking out loud to myself yet again, so who really knows.* Akira placed his head on the pillow and thought of Jake Johnson until he fell asleep. *Is this what it feels like to be a fangirl?* Then he drifted in the land of dreams.

• • •

The second that Akira fell asleep, he was in Jake's dreams. *Wow that was fast. I wonder why...* Akira was in an airport terminal. JFK from the looks of it. There were hundreds of people. They had the creepy shadow faces just like the other times. He started pushing through the shadow faced strangers. There was eerie heavy metal guitars playing out of the airport terminal's speakers. There were fast paced drums following. It sounded familiar, but nothing that Akira listened to. The metal music made him run faster. *How big can a dream be?* An announcement said: "All passengers with drum kits, your flight is going to be at terminal 5A". Akira ran to terminal 5A. When he arrived there were drum kits everywhere, then he spotted Jake next to a kit Akira has played before.

He was in a jacuzzi placed in the middle of the waiting area. His drum kit was dispersed around the tub. Angela was in the hot tub with him. "YO Akira! My dude! What's up? Did you know I'm going to be playing New England Metal Hardcore Festival? How sick is that?" Jake said through a big grin. All of the other drummers in the area had shadow faces. It reminded Akira of when they had those crime TV shows and the witness talks about something but they're blackened out to protect their identity.

"So where's the rest of the band dude?" Akira asked that rather than about the illogically placed jacuzzi. Jake's face suddenly went from calm to panic. He began looking around hastily. He jumped out.

"What the hell? Cody, Garrett, Billy! They should all be here.." Akira was wondering about if Jake was really dreaming this at this exact moment. He wished he could wake up and go check then come back. He thought about how he made that portal in Brent's dream. There certainly wasn't anything about that in any of the lucid dreaming articles.

"I'm sorry, but it's time to go now." Angela said who was magically out of the hot tub and her appealing bathing suit. Now she was dressed up nice like she was going to prom or something. Jake looked intently into his girlfriend's eyes.

"But why.." he said, with a tear in his eye. A plane took off from the terminal right beside them. "Damnit, look what I've done now. I ruined everything!" Jake, or at least "Dream Jake" looked very upset. Akira wondered if there was anything he could do. Then he noticed throughout the airport, fires broke out. Shadowy faced beings spontaneously combusted. Planes exploded.

Akira didn't want to be a part of Jake's dream anymore. He just wanted his friend to be happy. Then a floating dimensional rip opened up before his eyes. Inside, Akira saw Jake's practice space. He was with his band. Cody, Garrett and Billy were all in the practice space with him. They had beads of sweat dripping from their hair and rolling down their bodies. They just finished a full set list practice. They all looked too tired to speak, when Jake stood up from behind the drum kit. His shirt was off and he still looked like he just got out of the shower.

"Listen guys. Thank you all so much. That was such a killer jam sesh. We got a lot done. Even if we don't make it anywhere, I'm still having the time of my life." Akira realized that this was back two years ago a little after the band formed. Jake was just getting over his first big depression and heartbreak before he met Angela.

Akira looked into this good memory that he never experienced. Was his mind fabricating this? Or was this actually an event that transpired in Jake's life? He was struck with utter fascination. He reached out and touched the portal. It faded until it was nothing. Just like when you turned off one of those old TV sets, you could see the last flicker of electricity dissipate. Then, just like in the dinosaur nightmare with Brent, the images in the portal came to life--or so to speak. Cody, Garrett and Billy were all in the airport terminal and the rampant fires were gone. It was as if they were never even burned at all. Planes seamlessly put themselves back together.

Jake's face displayed little surprise and a lot of joy. He hugged all of them, instantly accepting the dream logic. Then they started to play one of their band's songs right at the airport. A mic stand

teleported in front of Cody, who grabbed it. The band began playing their instruments simultaneously just like the starting track on
their self-titled EP. "Hello, we're Animus Apart and we're here to
bring metal to the masses! 1-2-3-4!"

Akira found that no matter where he went in the terminal,
the music was always the same volume. And when he tried leaving
through the doors they were all locked. He wandered throughout
the terminal listening to Animus Apart's set while experimenting
in different ways. He discovered he could teleport most small ob-
jects he could think of into the dream. Unfortunately, it left him
feeling a little strained after each attempt. Akira finished his series
of tests when he teleported Amy into the dream. Her face was a
shadow. It was one of the creepiest things he had ever seen. He
held his hands out and tried focusing. His hands started jittering
like an addict that went cold turkey. Then they began shaking like
they were hit by powerful winds. When he tried taking the shadows that enveloped her face away with his mind, he suddenly lost
consciousness.

CHAPTER 10

MAY 30*TH*

AKIRA STRETCHED HIS ARMS. IT was a rough hangover. Or was it? *I don't remember drinking last night*...he slid his feet off the bed. Jake appeared in his doorway for what seemed like a couple of minutes. Akira couldn't place his finger on it, but he felt like he had to tell Jake something.

"Hey, breakfast is ready. C'mon up man." Jake said, disappearing from the doorway. Akira went up. Cody was looking intently into his phone at the table. Jake was sitting down petting their cat, Raymond. Raymond the Cat meowed and rubbed against Jake's leg. It's plan to seduce the human before attacking the delicious meat on the counter was only just beginning.

The meat was bacon and sausage being cooked by Joe Johnson. Cody and Jake's dad. "Mornin' Akira the lady killa," Joe said without turning around. He was frying eggs now. He brought the food to the table.

"Is Mom at work?" Cody asked while putting his phone away and replacing it with a fork.

"Yup, she had to open at the diner today," Joe said. "You know, with Summer coming up soon, I thought we could all hop on a plane and go away for a bit. How's that sound?" Jake woohoo'd and Cody clapped and whistled.

"That sounds great dad!" Cody said in an excited tone.

"Whaddya think Akira?" Joe said, taking note of Akira's puzzled expression. "Huh? Oh yeah that sounds awesome Mr. J. I'd be honored to come."

Akira was really focusing on one of the words Mr. J had said. Plane. It was bringing back the memories of his dream piece by piece. He was thinking about that and connecting the dots the entire breakfast. His only other task was getting the breakfast into his mouth without missing. While Akira was deep in thought, Cody was looking at him with a worried face.

• • •

7:20 AM MAY 31ˢᵀ, BLACKSTONE, VIRGINIA

A man with shaggy brown hair down to his shoulders and untamed facial hair that encompassed most of his neck and face was staring at a tray of food.

Philip Anthony Stone was eating McDonald's in a booth by himself. Or at least he was trying to. He had been there for an hour already. His meal was half-finished. It was warm and humid outside. He wiped the sticky sweat from his forehead.

"Daddy can I get another hashbrown?" A small girl asked with innocent shyness a few booths over. "Sure thing sweet pea. Wait here." The father figure got up and walked around to the counter. Phil was on edge. When the father got up he flinched and looked away as if he hadn't been eavesdropping. The man took no notice.

Phil had only been out for a week. But the nightmares now were so much worse than the ones before. The other ones were sporadic, dynamic. They were leftovers from his tragic adolescence. But this one has been constant and static. New. Fresh, and torturous.

It's the same dream every time. The only thing that changes is how Phil wakes up. Sometimes it's cold sweat. Sometimes it's an unwanted erection. But every single time, the last few sentences that were said in his dream haunts him all morning. Sometimes he can even see the words that were said floating like subtitles scratched into his eyeballs. Laced into his eyelids.

I need you to do something for me. I know what you did. I know what you are. The only person who can help you is me. Go to New York. We're all capable of redemption with a little assistance.

• • •

JUNE 1ST

The air was cool. It was like the wind decided to give up and go away for a while. Akira took his hand and dragged it across the granite letters.

Lin Kishimoto 1978-2020

"Such an angelic human being was she, that God decided to take this young angel early." The priest had said. Out of all of his friends, only the Johnson family attended her funeral. Akira preferred this, because his mom was buried all the way out in Queens. He didn't want to hassle anyone to go make the trip even though he knew most of his friends were good enough where they wouldn't feel bothered. At the same time, Akira also didn't want to deal with all of the "I'm sorry for your loss"es and all the condolences given because in the end it didn't do anything. Akira took some comfort knowing people were willing to help him out, but it saved him effort not having to deal with that. Naturally, he would deal with those things over the next few months anyway.

Many of Lin's colleagues were still there to fill in the void of sympathy. Some he knew, most he didn't. If Akira didn't know any better, he'd wonder if they all loved and respected her as much as it seemed; or if it was just tradition and formalities. But he did know better. His mom was intelligent and caring. He doubted more than a handful of people ever disliked her in her entire life.

"Well," he began backing away from the headstone. "I should probably get to school. You'd be mad if I was too late. By the way, Dad called. He was the one to tell me the news. He wants me to find him. I know I'm short a parent these days, but I don't think I want to see him. Not after what he did to you. I just.. I..don't know what to do anymore. Or what to believe. You're probably not even listening or capable of doing so. But if you are, just know that I love and miss you every single day." The image of the headstone began to fade, distorted by tears that did not drip. Akira wiped them before they did and then left. ·

• • •

Akira arrived at school two hours late. His mind wasn't on his education anyway. The logical assumption he reached was: If thinking about someone is all I have to do to enter their dreams, then what about if I thought about my mom. Nothing had happened. And so he went to visit her grave for the first time instead. Now he was in a miserable high school learning about nothing. The contempt he felt was only matched by his disappointment. *Couldn't my subconscious at least muster up a fake version of her for me? What's the point of even trying in school? My mom won't be there when I graduate. She won't be there if I get married. She won't ever be there again.* At these thoughts Akira began tearing up once more helplessly.

Without a sound he wiped his eyes and got up from the classroom and left. The teacher didn't say anything. He proceeded to the main lobby and went to leave. "Excuse me, you can't just leave. You need to get a parent to sign you out with a note!" exclaimed the sentry posted at the main entrance. Akira simply sneered. Red eyes and tears still streaming, he only looked at the chubby lady with curly hair and then pushed his way out the doors. "You need a note to wear that much damn lipstick," he muttered to himself outside. Then he drove himself to the place he now called home.

• • •

Several mix drinks and bowl packs later Akira was watching old television re-runs beside his unanswered phone. Cody trudged in and tossed Akira's backpack on his bed next to him. "Looks like you forgot something," Cody said with a forced smile. He looked at the table which looked like a battleground between half-empty bottles of liquor and baggies of marijuana. "Maybe you should relax with all that shit dude."

"HHHHHHHAAA. Me? Is this real life?" Akira said in a slur. "Cody Johnson telling me not to party?" Akira boomed with laughter. Cody felt like that laughter could transmute into hysterical crying at any second.

"A party is more than one person my man. You got me worried."

"It's not what it looks like. I'm not doing this to escape. I'm just distracting myself."

"Aren't those the same thi-"

"Have you ever seen *Arrested Development*? This show is like twenty years old but it is HILL-LARY-IS!"

Cody was looking down at the floor. The empty bottles looked like a small army trying to take Akira down. Like in *King Kong*, they would surround him, then transport him into New York City.

"Listen man, just relax for the rest of the night. Don't let my parents find out how fucked up you are right now. And if you need anything, please let me know. I'll be right upstairs."

"Of course!" Akira said tilting his last drink of the night up towards Cody. He watched him disappear then he resumed his comedic distraction. After a few episodes he got tired and shut off the TV. He tried to sleep but couldn't. He started thinking about his mom. Then he began to think of Amy and he became sad and horny, which was also interchangeable with his loneliness. *How could she do this to me? How could she just throw me away and run away with some douchebag Prince Charming?* He wanted to fight her new boyfriend. He felt like he had enough displaceable rage that he could actually win. He imagined being on top of Jack who he had only seen pictures of on the internet, some by himself, some kissing the girl he was in love with and fell asleep next to only a few months ago. The first few punches would be supported by the snake-like qualities Jack possessed. Did you know Satan originally took the form of a snake? Then ultimately Akira knew he could somehow pretend Jack was the one to blame for his mother's death, and at that point he had imagined Jack would be missing some teeth and quite bloody.

It was a weird feeling. He also kind of wished Brent or one of his friends would try fighting him too. He had so much anger inside he didn't even care if he lost. Life was punching him in the face, so why shouldn't other people get the chance too? Then he was back to thinking about Amy. The taste of her lips. The way she maneuvered her tongue. How she sounded when she laughed.

One time Akira was trying to say something and jumbled up his words. The end result was: "It was the sick".

Somehow the simple accidental insertion of the word "the" had her booming with laughter for what seemed like forever. It was such a beautiful, youthful laugh. As long as her laugh sounded the same, Amy would never age. He drifted into sleep. Recalling all the other memories they shared where she laughed. What he would do to hear that laugh again. He guessed he'd do nearly anything.

• • •

It was dark. Akira noticed a familiar looking beach and walked over to it. There she was, sitting under the light of the moon. The moon acted as a spotlight illuminating Amy on a lawn chair. She was reading a novel. It was *50 Shades of Grey*. "I don't even know if this is my dream or not anymore," Akira said to no one specifically. Amy jumped up off the lawn chair.

"Akira… is that you?"

"You know it is. Didn't expect me huh?"

"Well.. it has been a while."

"I know, I haven't seen you in forever. I've missed you quite a lot."

"Well, I meant in my dreams, but in real life too. I'm so sorry about your---"

Akira held up his hand. The universal symbol for "stop" worked.

His eyes were frowning as much as his mouth was. He turned one corner of his mouth upwards. The result was an awkwardly fake smile.

"It's just so nice to.. look at you. In person. I've looked at your pictures a lot. The picture of us together was my phone's background until a week ago. You look beautiful in all of your pictures, but the pixels just don't do your beauty justice. Your essence is so invigorating, nothing can capture that."

She laughed. It was small, but it sounded real. It was the greatest thing he heard in weeks. Then she smiled her smile with the most kissable lips he had ever known. "You've always had a way with words. That's why I liked you so much."

The word "like" stung almost as much as the past tense version she used.

Your words are daggers, they make me bleed but they are not forever.

"I guess Jack had a way with more than just words."

Her smile immediately dropped into a frown.

He kicked himself in his head for ruining the moment, but also simultaneously felt pride in bringing the homewrecker up.

"No. I don't know what it is, but I'm just drawn to him,"

She walked towards him and put her hands on his. They were colder than he remembered. "Akira, Jack kissed me while I was on vacation. That was where I met him. I am so sorry." Her face was apologetic. Her eyes were pleading. She felt better immediately after getting that off her chest. Akira could feel it. He could sense it. Suddenly his entire world began spinning. He felt drunk again. *Jack really was a homewrecker then..*

"I have to go now. But before I do," he nearly leapt towards Amy and grabbed her head. He moved his face in closer and instead of resisting, she closed her eyes and let him kiss her. Akira kissed like no one she ever met. The passion he put into every kiss could be used to describe what kind of person he was. It was one of the things she missed the most. When the feeling of his lips suddenly became absent, she opened her eyes and Akira was gone.

CHAPTER 11

JUNE 2ND

IT WASN'T THAT STRANGE OF a morning. After all, it wasn't the first morning Akira woke up crying. Amy did hook up with Jack before they broke up. His mind kept playing with this information, accessing it, questioning the possibility and how it could have happened. Maybe it was his own dream? No, then he wouldn't remember it so vividly. What could have been done to prevent that? Why wasn't he good enough? He asked himself but he really knew he wasn't anywhere near her league to begin with. Besides, what's done is done right?

He had been lying in his bed staring at the ceiling for over an hour already, when his phone began vibrating. It was a text tone. Amy had texted him.

"Hey."

One simple word, but it made his head spin again. Just seeing her name on his phone gave him anxiety, excitement, sadness. He actually let out a whimper. It was too much to be coincidental. He responded and she asked him how he was. She said she missed him. Akira lied and said he was well. He didn't know why she bothered to text him. He still knew she was with her boyfriend. Life goes on.

Akira began seeing a Psychiatrist the next day. Dr. Joshua Lang was the name of the man on the other side of the desk. At first

Akira was quiet. He discredited the possibility of feeling any better after talking to this stranger with a degree. But by the end of the session he got a decent amount off his chest. Stuff he couldn't say to Cody or Jake because they were his best friends. But this well paid stranger was just that, a stranger. For reasons Akira didn't fully understand, it made it easier to dump his problems onto this person. He wondered if it was because he didn't care about burdening this man or because this man likely didn't actually care about him. That meant no real pity.

At the end of the session Dr. Lang had said: "The way I've seen it since I was child, cause I too, lost a parent at a young age, was that life is like a mountain range. It goes up and it goes down. No matter what, you'll always be going back up and you'll always be going back down. But when you're at the lowest point, you can't see the top of the mountain. Therefore, you don't really believe it's there. You have to stay strong and resilient in order to continue through the mountain range. There will always be highs and lows that await us."

"What happens if we can't handle the lows?" Akira asked.

"Our emotions are always there for a reason. They can be difficult to deal with, but it's a necessary task. We cannot hide from what we feel or distract ourselves. Instead, we should talk to our emotions. Confront them head on. Pretend Sadness is sitting beside you, ask it 'Why have you come? Why are you here? What is your purpose? Hello, Depression. I hear what you're saying but it will be okay.' This way, we externalize our issues, because when they are kept inside they're harder to deal with."

Akira thought that over for a long time after paying the man and leaving. Maybe it was only in the guy's job description to care. He gave some good advice regardless. But Akira still liked the roller coaster analogy. In that analogy, you can't see the twists and turns until they're happening. Also, when thinking about life, you want to puke. Just like a spiral roller coaster. Perhaps that was just the new Akira's cynical analysis speaking though. Although Akira did have to confess that he felt a little bit better.

Later that night, Akira thought of Dr. Lang before he went to sleep. How ironic would it be for him to get into his own psychiatrist's head? But the attempt failed. Akira woke up from a dreamless sleep. He wrote this in his newly created dream journal.

• • •

6/3/20

Dream Entry 4: Tried dreamwalking in my psychiatrist Dr. Lang's dreams. It didn't work. Must figure out what variable made it ineffective. Age? Distance? Health? Smarter than my other "Subjects"? Will continue trying to learn more.

He had begun calling his ability dreamwalking shortly after his encounter with Brent in the football stadium. He wrote this event out and entered it as his second entry.

• • •

6/6/20

Dream Entry 6: Last night I toyed around with changing the scenery in dreams. I entered my foster father's dreams. Mr. Johnson has always treated me right. I didn't want to overstep my bounds. However, if I have inhuman powers, or supernatural powers I have to learn to control them. Just like in the comics! Except

I don't exactly know if I can save the world or anything haha. Anyways, that's my justification.

Mr. Johnson was dreaming of racing a car. It was a drag race. I watched as Joe Johnson's vehicle lurched forward, leaving a plume of smoke in its wake. The audience's anticipation rose to a shriek as Joe finished ahead of the rival racer. I couldn't see his face, but I bet he was smiling. I decided to try to change the dream with my own willpower. If you didn't know any better, you would think I was lucid dreaming and taking control of my own dream. But nope, I'm literally controlling someone else's dream. Anyway, I changed the entire dream. All I did was close my eyes and imagine that it wasn't a drag race anymore. Now it was a NASCAR race. Suddenly, when I opened my eyes WHAM. The entire track was transformed from a line to a circuit. There were multiple cars on the track now instead of just two. An instantaneous screech of noise burst out. ZROOOOOOOOOOM! Mr. Johnson was still ahead of the pack.

Next, I had to find something else out. I waited in the pit area with Cody and Jake (dream versions of course) until Mr. J arrived. He finished in first place. He was absolutely ecstatic.

"Boys! I'm so glad you're all here!!" Mr. J said, face gleaming, "Can you believe it?!".

"We certainly can!" I answered.

"Say Mr. J, how about we all go to the diner to celebrate!" As I made the suggestion I gave a slight push with my words. I used some of my energy behind that suggestion, supporting it with a force of energy I can't quite explain.

"Well Akira, my friends can call me JJ. And the diner sounds like a fantastic idea!"

Shortly after, I left the dream. The next day when we got back from school, Mr. Johnson (or JJ if you're a friend) said he wanted to take us all to the diner. After we got there, I told him it was kind of random for him to want the diner so badly. "I don't know; I was just feelin' it all day I guess!" was his answer. I would have asked him what he dreamt, but for now I think it's safe to assume he didn't remember any of it.

. . .

6/18/20

Dream Entry 8: I entered Ian Mckinley's dreams. For some reason it took a lot of my energy and focus to even arrive in his dreams (after meditation I was drenched with sweat) but when I got there he was dreaming he was playing drinking games with his friends. Without letting myself be seen, I used my ability to get the principal of the school to come and break the party up. I managed to do what I call "dream digging" again, to find a memory of Ian's older brother Jack beating on him. This memory wasn't really hidden; I think Ian must have thought about it a lot. Possibly when he's at the gym, or when he's bullying others. Doesn't matter. I brought it up, but without making his older brother appear, I simply managed to affect how Ian felt back then. In his rage, he punched the principal in the face. As he did it I closed my eyes and thought about the punch. I focused real hard until I felt so tired I'd collapse.

I was hoping he would attempt to go to school and assault our beloved principal without knowing why. I'm not sure why, but I failed in this. I have a theory that it could be because Mr. Johnson would want to take everyone out to the dinner more than Ian would want to punch a principal he doesn't see anymore.

Either way I think I'm learning a lot about these powers I have...even the stuff I don't know I think I can figure out with enough "test trials" and theories. The only thing I don't even have so much as a theory on is, why do I have this power..?

• • •

7/2/20

Dream Entry 9: I made love to Amy again. Both in her dreams and in real life. She cheated on her boyfriend with me. I dreamwalked into her dream and we had sex. Then later that week she hit me up. I don't know if my dreamwalking influenced her to contact me in real life and be as flirty as she was, but I do know I don't feel bad. I have no regrets. Jack didn't care when she was with me, why should I care about him? Honestly I haven't been this happy since.. well.. you know.

When I was in Amy's dreams she told me she loved me. She didn't say anything of the sort when we did it in real life.

Unfortunately, at the time of this week I was also in a relationship. I rebounded without even knowing it to my closest female friend at the time. Her name was Allison. I don't know why all the most beautiful women in my life have "a" lettered names, but it is what it is. Allison liked me for a long time. I wasn't sure of it until I kissed her in her backyard. My heart thought she was right for me. Maybe she was, but I was nowhere near as over Amy as I had thought. When Amy contacted me a week and half into our relationship, I couldn't resist answering. I was under a spell. I was in love. I broke up with Allison the day after I cheated on her. It sucked. At first I regretted doing her dirty like that, but my God how could I honestly say I regretted kissing Amy one more time?

Seeing her? It was so much better in real life than in my dreams. Fuck.

When Amy said goodbye I wrapped my arms around her. I held her close and kissed her head. I could feel it in my bones. This would be the last time she would ever be mine. She looked up at me, evidently worried by my silence. With her head tilted towards mine, I grabbed her face and kissed it. All of my passion went into that kiss as well as all of my fears. The euphoria from both times we slept together stayed with me for several days. I graduated High School that week and didn't even care about the heat during practice. Soon, I wouldn't care about anything anymore at all. I could sense the disaster that was on its way.

· · ·

8/8/20

Dream Entry 11: As expected, Amy cut off contact with me. She left my life as quickly as she came back into it. I don't know if my foresight about her actions made it better or worse, but I spent the first half of my summer crying and hating my life. I drank and smoked and got fucked up. Anything to get my mind off of how the two women I loved the most in the world were now dead to me. One was a familial love and actual death, the other romantic, and figuratively dead. I kept hoping to run into her places for God knows what reasons, but we never did. She told Jack she cheated on him and he took her back. I have no one. And in a way, it was what I deserved. I lost a good friend too, and I told Allison I understood if she hates me from then on.

Then I decided to turn my attention back to dreamwalking. I hadn't done it since Amy stopped answering my messages. After several "experiments" I deduced that distance is a major factor in my ability to dreamwalk and how powerful I was in the person's dreams. In the Johnson's dreams while they were home, I was practically a demigod in their dreams. But one weekend Jake and his girlfriend went away upstate and I couldn't enter his dreams. I tried several times that weekend just in case he was awake when I tried. I tried Cooper while he was away for something baseball related. Everything I tried to do made me feel like I was going to pass out. I barely managed to summon an item in his dream. I also found out that the night I messed with Ian Mckinley, he beat the crap out of his older brother.. instead of the principal. Interesting.. Ian Mckinley also lives on the edge of town. There are always a lot of variables in play. But at least I won't have a boring Summer. Love and miss you so much Mom!

. . .

8/24/20

Dream Entry 14: I guess these dream entries ended up being pretty therapeutic. I didn't know writing out my emotions could help me feel better, but that's exactly what happened. College orientation is soon, so I guess this is it for my so-called "dream journal." Thank you for helping me feel better. Hopefully I'll find time to write more. Maybe craft a fiction story too. That'd be cool.

. . .

AUGUST 26TH

Philip Stone was walking down Interstate 95 hitchhiking. Again. Thus far, he had only been able to successfully hitch two rides. The first was a friendly Christian mom who drove him onto the I-95. She dropped him off at a rest stop when she noticed how often he glanced at her breasts. He watched the Toyota Prius with the **Keep Christ in Christmas** and the **Lookout! Jesus is always watching** bumper stickers zoom out and back onto the exit ramp. Jesus had binoculars in the second bumper sticker and Philip thought it made him look more like a peeping Tom.

Philip was hungry, so he was forced to loiter outside asking for money to eat. After three hours, he made almost four dollars. Enough for him to eat *something* that night. If he could, he'd stay in a town or city for a few days to a week. He'd work an odd job, usually consisting of picking up trash or washing dishes to make money for food. But eventually, the nightmares started back up again. Now he couldn't afford to work on his way up north.

The second driver was a truck driver. The truck driver's name was Ronald Feinberg. And he was drunk. Philip watched with great curiosity as the man drank beer after beer and engaged him in small talk.

"So what's a man like yourself doing walkin' up this here interstate anyway? Is it a loooooove story?" He snorted in self-appraised laughter.

Punch this freak in his face, his intoxicated dribble and his driving will slow us down. WE NEED TO GET TO THE CITY THAT NEVER SLEEPS.

Philip began experiencing one of the headaches he got every now and then. He convinced himself when he was let out of the asylum that it was normal.

"No siree! My momma lives in NY and she's dying and I gots to see her!" Philip replied. He began focusing on the smog shooting out of the top of the truck. He watched its reflection in the rearview mirror of the truck. The black smoke rose up and dissipated into the sky.

Wow Phil, look at all the pollution this neanderthal is releasing into the environment. All of those animals you love are going to die because of this asshole.

"Nooo. The birdies.." Philip muttered. His hands were clasped over his head. Ronald was still talking conversationally, seemingly unconcerned with the notion of whether or not his passenger was listening or not. Although Philip did hear his last sentence. "Hold on now chum, we've got to stop and get some gas."

Philip watched Ron get out and go to fill up his gas tank. As he stepped out of the vehicle, a beer can tried following him out. Phil also noted that Ron left his keys in the cabin of the truck. *You know what to do.* The politely violent voice said.

"But Kenneth," Philip pleaded out loud. His headache got worse.

But nothing you fuck stick, do you wanna hafta see him again?

Philip hopped over to the driver's side and plugged in the keys. The truck roared to life. Philip didn't have any truck driving experience, let alone that much driving experience in general. He decided he had to learn quickly when he saw Ron in the rearview mirror running to the truck. The whole truck lurched forward. Philip heard a clang as Ron smacked his fist hard into the back of the truck as it rushed out of the parking lot.

Ron reached into his pockets to call the police. Sadly, he realized his phone was inside his truck. All he had was his wallet. Running fast for the first time since high school gym, Ronald Feinberg went into the rest stop gas station for help.

Philip Anthony Stone drove about 150 miles until he was on the outskirts of Trenton, New Jersey. Arriving at a junkyard, he made a deal to sell the truck for scrap metal. The worker wanted proof that Phil had ownership of the vehicle, but at suggestion by the angry voice inside his head, he offered to only take half the price if they kept it "their little secret." Phil left the lot an hour later with $2,400. He realized without the title it was highly likely he got ripped off, but this amount of money was sufficient. He was back on track, and his master would be pleased.

CHAPTER 12

AUGUST *31*ST

AKIRA WAS READING ON A train to New York City. He was on his way to college orientation at the New York City College of Technology. In between reading chapters of *The Bourne Identity*, Akira would stop and think about college. He was going to miss Cody and Jake and all of his other friends. *Will I make new friends? Maybe. Will I have new experiences? Definitely.*

Akira had become cocky about his dreamwalking abilities. But curiosity still encouraged him to learn more. He felt the possibilities were endless. Because of this, Akira reviewed his dream journal every single day. He had accumulated over twenty entries. He blushed as he imagined using his powers on an attractive girl to come back to his college dorm.

It was a boiling hot day. Akira left Penn Station to grab something to eat while the heat bounced off of the tall skyscrapers like a magnifying glass.

Akira had only been to the Big Apple a few times in his life. Every time except for his last visit, Akira went with his mom. The last time he was here Jake and Cody dragged him to a concert. Akira ended up having an awesome time even though he didn't know the bands and they all missed the last outgoing train.

Despite his fret about the subway, Akira found it to be way less intimidating than he suspected. One question to the bored tick-et booth lady and he knew where to go. The subway was filled with busy in-a-rush people from every corner of the world. Akira wouldn't even bet a dollar on who actually lived here in the city aside from the occasional bums. He supposed that the other residents could probably pick each other out from the flock of tourists though.

He bumped into a man in a suit and turned saying "Oops I'm sorry!". The man did not turn or answer, he either did not hear Akira or did not care.

Akira soon entered the college's massive building and found his way into the auditorium. Many of the seats were already filled and many of the faces were blank. Akira sat next to an attractive redhead. A long haired stranger filed in the same row and sat next to Akira's other side. After a moment of tapping his knees, he be-gan to speak.

"All of these people look so smart. I bet they would cry if they ever inhaled a puff of weed. Are you like that my man?" Asked the long haired stranger with his head slightly turned to gauge Akira's reaction.

"No, I don't think so." Akira said honestly.

In the corner of his eye he could see the redhead listening, but not necessarily eavesdropping.

"Good. You look like you've seen some *shit*. You're more inter-esting than any of these spoiled brats already." The man took out a cigarette and put it in his mouth. "My name's Ray."

Akira looked at Ray with eyes that seemed to scan him. "My name's Akira. I'm from eastern Long Island. I also don't think you can smoke that in here."

"Ha! I could have believed you were from around here or NYC judging by your rough edges." He said, ignoring Akira's last comment.

"You give me too much credit. It's nice to meet you." Akira said through an uncomfortable laugh.

Three rows behind them someone was leaning at the edge of their seat. They focused all of their energy to overhear Akira's conversation amongst the chatter flooding the room.

"So his name is Akira.. well this should make things interesting." The man with an army crew cut said while twirling a toothpick in his mouth.

A man walked up to the podium on the stage and went behind the mic. The well dressed, well-kept man, began the boring orientation.

"...And that just about finishes up our policy on sexual harassment and how serious we are about maintaining a strict student friendly-environment..."

"Well, if he really wanted a student friendly environment, I think he should allow some of the hotter babes that teach to sexually harass those who are willing!" Ray said snickering. Akira offered a friendly smile but thought about how his mom used to get hit on by some students.

"They called me the hot Asian lady! Don't these kids know that they're well, kids?!" Lin had said once. Akira thought she was so innocent even though she was the adult and he was the kid.

"Shut up," the redhead next to Akira said with little interest.

Ray leaned forward to look past Akira.

He looked at her inquisitively for a moment then said "So she can speak!"

"Yes. I just chose silence over speaking with you." She said with zero inflection.

"Well well well! I was wondering how many sexist comments it would take for you to step outside of your shell! I expected a harsher version of shut up though. Perhaps 'shut the fuck up' or the classic 'shhhhhhh'."

The redhead looked back at him with one eyebrow raised.

"You're weird. Now be quiet before we get kicked out."

Akira chuckled, but had the vaguest feeling that someone was watching him. He couldn't get past it. Looking behind him, he saw a bunch of faces attentively watching the stage. Occasionally one of the pairs of eyes would look down and meet his with a sneer.

"Not until you tell me and my boy Akira your name!"

"Fine. My name is Lauren. Is that good enough?"

"Sitting a seat over from you isn't even good enough baby doll but that's okay!"

And that's how Akira met his first two friends at New York City's College of Technology.

• • •

Akira got a tour of the school with a bunch of students. Then they showed him to his dorm room. His RA seemed nice enough. Inside his dorm room a man with long hair and piercings was sitting on one of three beds. The kid's eyes were hidden behind thick bangs. Despite this, his hair still wasn't longer than Ray's was.

The Room Advisor continued with the rest of the group to bring them to their dorm rooms. "Yo what's up. My name is Cory dawg. How about you?" He asked while standing up to give Akira a friendly handshake. Akira took note of how tight his pants were. He donned a studded belt, and a black bandana littered with skulls. "I'm guessing your last name isn't dog right? My name is Akira Kishimoto."

They shook hands. "Deadass! Yooo my full name is Cory Owens. And your new name is AK-47!" Then Cory pulled Akira in chest to chest and slapped him on the back with his other hand. Akira took a moment to understand where his new nickname derived from. He didn't mind it too much, as long as only Cory was calling him that.

"So AK-47. Let's hear the life story! No, wait. Our third roomie will be here any minute. That or in a hot minute."

"Uh, what's the difference?" Akira asked earnestly.

"A hot minute is longer. Could be almost an hour mahniggah!"

Akira was unsure how to demonstrate how uncomfortable the street lingo made him feel. He didn't have to because there was a knock at his door.

"Yo yo yo what's up ho!" Cory said while answering the door.

"Are you autistic?" Ray asked while entering the room. Cory turned his head and mumbled the word no. "Hey Akira, sup man. I switched into your room."

"Greeat," Akira said sarcastically then laughed. Ray matched his laugh. Ray and Cory introduced themselves to each other.

Akira was already analyzing the very plain room. "I claim that bed!" He said pointing towards the one on the far corner. It had the smallest dresser, but the most privacy and a window next to it.

Corey walked over to the bed on the other side of the room. "It's all good dawg, my posters will fit perfectly above this one!"

They talked about their life stories. Hailing from Idaho, Corey's tale was one of rebellion. His parents were disappointed that he didn't like sports. Akira felt as though Corey was exaggerating the extent of his parent's disappointment, at least until he got up to the part where his parents found out he smokes cigarettes. This was when Corey was at the delicate and impressionable age of twelve. Corey claimed that was when his father hit him for the first time. By the end of Corey's story, he understandably sought salvation and escape from his parents and ended up going to school hundreds of miles away.

Ray's story wasn't as crazy as Akira expected. Ray simply got into trouble a lot. He got into a bunch of fights and even impregnated a girlfriend when he was eighteen. "Yeah I pay child support, so what!" Ray said, embarrassed when Corey asked what was good with the kid.

After Ray was finished, he sat on his new bed and stared at Akira patiently. Corey was twirling a cigarette in his hands awaiting Akira's back story as well. *Great, I'm the only one in the dorm who doesn't smoke cigarettes. Greaaaaat.*

"So. I was born and raised on eastern Long Island. I live about two hours from where we are now. I like comics, videogames and girls. My father hasn't been in my life for years. And my mom passed away this year." Ray kept watching without a change of expression. Corey's face turned into a frown. "I'm sorry to hear that homie."

Akira forced a half smile and thanked him for his condolences. "Anyway, that's about the jist of it."

"That's it?" Ray asked. "That's it," Akira answered. "For now."

Akira suddenly realized he was acting pseudo-mysteriously.

"Good enough for me!" Corey said.

They talked for a few hours then wandered around the campus together for a while. At the end of the night, Akira decided he could have ended up with worse roommates. He supposed Corey and Ray weren't Cody and Jake, but he could have been stuck with a Brent or Tyler.

Akira took out his iPod and headphones. His eccentric room-mates were now preparing for sleep, as was he.. in a way. Akira was going to Dreamwalk into one of their dreams. *Is it rude to do so even though I just met them? No, It's not sex. I have powers that must remain a secret, I'd never even be able to receive consent. As long as I'm not manipulating their actions, I'm just a witness to their dreams* Akira reasoned inside his head. *But which one shall I dreamwalk into first, Ray or Corey?* He flipped a coin. It was heads. Akira had designated heads for Ray prior to the coin flip. *Well Chum, guess it's you first.* Akira sat up looking at Ray, whose bed was in the middle of the room. He was already sleeping.

Akira put on God Is An Astronaut, an instrumental band that helped him feel at ease. In his testing, Akira found that music could help influence how quickly he began dreamwalking. One time while listening to hardcore rap it took him over an hour to dreamwalk. Death metal yielded no better results.

As piano, guitar, drums and bass melted together, Akira detected himself leaving his body. The first time he actually felt himself leaving his own body Akira freaked out. By the time he started dreamwalking in that person's dreams he was terrified he would get trapped.

Akira slipped from his body into the mind of his new acquaintance no more than a few feet away. But then something new happened. Something that hasn't happened to Akira before, despite all of his trials.

PART III
DREAMWALKING INTERRUPTED!

...

CHAPTER 13

AKIRA WAS FINALLY ABLE TO use his eyes.. but he still did not see anything. It was pitch black. Akira immediately thought his eyes were still closed but they weren't. Never in his life had he ever seen such eternal darkness. When all of the lights are out in your house it's still not truly pitch black. Light has a way of seeping in through some crevice, some opening. It's never truly dark unless you're underground or in a building that was sealed off. *Where am I?* The darkness gave way to helplessness and Akira resisted a temptation to scream.

Suddenly without warning, Akira's feet were soaked. Bending his knees into a crouch, he realized he was up to his shins in...water? Before he could kneel down and drink or smell the liquid to be sure, he heard the sounds of motion in the liquid come from behind him. "Ray... is that you?"

The figure was still cutting through the water towards Akira.

"I guess you're weaker than I thought."

The strange voice said. It didn't sound like any of the voices Akira had heard earlier today. "Who are you? And where are we?" A moon bigger than any moon Akira has ever seen appeared out of nowhere, illuminating what appeared to be a swamp or bog filled with trees with extraordinary roots and misty rocks. Fog was present everywhere he looked, as though it would have been invisible without the moonlight. Akira now saw the outline of the figure who was walking towards him, except the figure was currently motionless.

"I had a feeling you would use your powers on the very first night. You probably just couldn't wait to have new guinea pigs. I bet you already used your powers on everyone you knew back home, huh?"

Akira was sweating. He didn't know if it was because of how creeped out he was, or how damp and humid the bog was. "Who the hell are you and what are you doing here?"

"Instead, I think I'll answer the question you *didn't* ask." Akira felt that the anonymous figure before him could of had his condescension cut with a knife, not totally unlike the fog. "I know this about you because I was like that my first semester of college too. But I always like to back up my statements too, so I checked some of your memories. Sorry, guess I forgot to ask first!" he said. Akira was thinking about how he was able to manipulate the memories of the people he was dreamwalking inside of. *Does that mean he entered my dreams, before I entered Ray's dream?*

"Anyway," the pretentious figure continued, "It's your lucky day. I only came here to warn you. I figure you're a smart kid. So by now you realize you're not the only one with this gift. Well, hate to break it to you, but we're not the only ones either."

"What?" Akira asked through his teeth. He didn't even consider the possibility. In the superman comics, there's only one Superman. Sure there's knock offs, but not everyone can do the things he could. In Spiderman, there wasn't a Spidey in every other town or county.

"Oh yeah. And when you use your powers, it's like sending out a beacon to those who are looking. Some people can even sense you when you're not using your powers. There's an organization who is looking for noobies just like yourself, ones who don't know shit about what they're doing."

"Who are you and why are you telling me this then? If what you say is true, aren't you risking your neck for me by using your powers?"

"Heh, perceptive brat huh?" Akira began walking towards the figure. "Well, there are ways to, let's say, weaken the beacon that goes out when you use your powers. I'll let you figure that out though." Akira was inches away from the figure but it was still just that. A black shadow standing up right. He put his hand on it---but it went completely through the figure. "Anyway, have fun in your roommate's head. You're already there, but I cut you off. His dream is going on around us as we speak. I'm sure we'll meet again, when you're a bit more..ready."

Akira looked around at the mist that surrounded him. "WAIIT!" Akira yelled, "Ready for what? STOP BEING SO VAGUE!" He was no longer worried that he might be yelling that back in the dorm room as well. Akira's voice simply echoed throughout the swamp, and faded away. Akira couldn't put his finger on it, but he knew that he was alone again. Almost as if to prove him right, crickets began chirping the night away.

• • •

There was a massive, overturned tree. Akira neared it, and two things piqued his interest. It was completely hollow and the second thing was a bright light at the end of the other side. Still disorientated by the stranger, Akira trotted into the log tunnel.

The fog inside the log was slowly beginning to dissipate. The swamp like smells began to fade away. Akira remembered just earlier that day, he left the subway and was overcome by rancid smells.

It smelled like a million animals all defecated and died where he stood. The pungent smell of filth, garbage and burnt fossil fuels maintained a strong hold on him, and then disappeared without a trace when he got to his new college.

Just like that, the swamp smell disappeared and was replaced by a fresher smell. The smell of the ocean. Saltwater and beaches. As he exited the hollow log, Akira was overwhelmed by sunlight. It was a sunny day at a beach with clearer water than Akira has ever seen in New York.

Sitting on a lawn chair with beer bottles surrounding him, Ray was lying in the shade of an umbrella. Despite not being able to see him, Akira knew it was him. Walking alongside his lawn chair, Akira noticed there was a kid on his lap. To surprise him further, Ray said "What's up roomie, how do you like my beach?"

"Your beach?" Akira asked. He noted what he assumed was Ray's kid's smile and serene face.

"Yeah," Ray said lighting a cigarette. "I come here when I'm stressed, pissed off, or whatever." Akira studied his face and watched him puff out smoke over his kid's head. Before he could say anything Ray answered his unwarranted comment before it was even said. "It's a dream, don't worry. I can smoke in front of my daughter if I want." No one Akira dreamwalked with has ever been this aware. Did he know Akira wasn't exactly a conventional figment of his dream?

"Is that why you're here Ray? Because you're stressed or angry or because you're trying to get away?"

"Maybe. I was never very good at any of this school stuff. I almost failed out of high school multiple times. Almost got left back too. If I didn't bribe people in my district, I wouldn't have had good enough grades senior year to get into here. Maybe I'm afraid they'll find out." Ray inhaled sharply. Then he blew Os with the smoke. "Doesn't really matter why I'm here though. Why are *you* here *chum?*"

Akira took a step back. He put his hands in front of his chest and then closed his eyes and smiled. He didn't know it, but he had inherited some of his mom's disarmingly subtle charm. "I really don't know, I guess it's just such a beautiful beach, what can I say!" He chuckled nervously. Perhaps his passed down gifts still needed some work.

Akira was too afraid to try to push Ray to do anything. He was too cautious to try to change the environment, or summon an item. Akira had to do something he had only done twice before. Leave the dream prematurely. It was for the best. Usually he wouldn't leave of his own free will, he would push his powers too much and pass out. But between Akira's encounter with the stranger and Ray's unusually high perception, he just wanted to get out and go to bed.

Akira closed his eyes and put his hands together like he was praying. Tilting his head forward, he cleared his mind of all thoughts. Akira began to fade away. Now he was in what he called "ghost form" where the dreamer can no longer see him.

"Akira...?" Ray called out. He leaned over the lawn chair and looked behind him and then shrugged as he looked directly where Akira was still standing, only now in a different realm? Dimension? Akira was still decently unsure what to call it. But from here, he also learned he could levitate. And fly! He couldn't do it very fast, but still *how awesome is that?* Akira had told himself. In order to get out of the dream from here, Akira had to leave the "scene" that is going on. Akira discovered wherever the dreamer is, was usually the center of the dream. However, he still found it the most entertaining to simply fly straight up.

Eventually the beach below him shrank until it disappeared from sight. Rising above a few layers of clouds, Akira finally saw the darkness above. When he first saw it he believed it was space, but now he knew it was simply where the dream ends. Once he reaches it, he will return back to real life again. Back to his *real* body.

Akira did just that until he opened one eye and was looking at his dorm room and roommates. Ray and Corey were still asleep. Corey was snoring. Ray wasn't facing Akira. Akira had a strong impulse to get up and walk over to Ray's other side to *guarantee* that he was sleeping. He resisted it, and thought about the stranger and the things he said. Akira remembered just about every word perfectly.

I had a feeling you would use your powers on the very first night. You probably just couldn't wait to have new guinea pigs. I bet you already used your powers on everyone you knew back home, huh?

• • •

After the weekend ended, classes began. Akira hadn't dared dreamwalk again. He was kind of terrified. Ray didn't seem to act like he remembered anything, or if he did he kept quiet about it. Naturally, Akira didn't inquire about it.

As each of his classes went on, he distracted himself by observing his classmates more so than usual. In all of his classes he grabbed a seat in the back. Throughout Freshman Seminar, Volleyball, Algebra, Western Civ and Literature he looked for anyone that could have been the other dreamwalker. Of course he only had a voice and taste of a condescending personality to go by, but he was still determined to level the playing field and find out who it was. Unfortunately, at a tech school, he soon learned many people seemed to have holier-than-thou personalities.

Akira was walking down a hallway a week later. He was on his way to a cafeteria when the girl named Lauren from orientation passed by him. She looked at him then looked away, but after passing him stopped once more.

"Um, it was Akira, right?"

"Huh? Oh-oh yeah," Akira answered while turning around. "Lauren. How are things?" Akira asked while being caught off guard. *She remembered your name. Imagine it was her?* The Akira inside his head said bluntly.

"They're good! I was kinda wondering if you'd want to come investigate one of the clubs with me.."

Akira waited to see if his stomach would rumble. It did not.

"Sure, what club were you thinking about?" he asked conversationally.

"Robotics! I've always wanted to build one. And our school has had some famous bot inventors come through here."

"Okay, sounds good to me. Let's go!"

He walked with her; the opposite direction of the school's cafe.

"I'll be honest, I'm surprised you remembered my name, let alone wanted me to accompany you. I definitely don't mind it though." he assured her.

"Well, I've never been too good at making friends. And I have heard that the president of the club could come on a little..strong. Couldn't hurt to have a familiar face with me ya know?"

Akira nodded. Robotics. He never cared too much for them, or the ever growing industry. But he supposed looking into joining a club on his spare time might be a good idea too.

Lauren was looking at down at her phone. Possibly reading a text, possibly looking up campus directions. Akira didn't intend on prying enough to find out.

Several moments went by kind of awkwardly until the duo pushed through the wooden door with a paper taped to it reading: **Robotic Engineering Club**.

The room was clearly used for tech classes, with long scarred wooden tables stretching across it in rows. There were nine people scattered across the room sitting at different tables, except for two in the front. Many of them had the appearances of your typical tech nerds. Glasses, pimples, and sweater vests. *Me and Lauren are the best looking people in here* Akira thought without a trace of modesty. Then he turned and saw a man who looked almost ten years older sitting at the teacher's desk in the room.

"And you two are..?" he asked with an eyebrow raised.

Akira noted with some jealously the way Lauren smiled when she recognized the not-so-nerdy-looking fellow behind the desk. Blushing, Lauren replied instantly. "My name is Lauren, and I'm interested in joining this club!"

A pasty redhead girl with freckles sneered. "Do you even know what this club is for?"

"Uh, yeah. Robotic engineering. It says it right there on the door. And on the board." She gestured with her head past the objectively attractive teacher to the chalkboard behind him. The teacher looked at Lauren from head to toe, then back up again. He smirked, then shifted his gaze to Akira. His smirk became a half frown.

"And you?"

"My name is Akira Kishimoto. I'd also like to see about joining this club."

The smirk returned. "And I am Sid Meyers," now it was a grin. "Pleasure to meet the both of you. I'm a junior here. This is my second year as the president of this club." *Holy shit, he's a student?*

"Are you two, well, you know.."

"None of your-" Akira said until Lauren answered "Nope, just friends!"

Akira awkwardly pretended as if he hadn't spoke at all. *Talk about coming on too strong* Akira thought with a ping of jealousy.

"Excellent! Excellent!" Sid exclaimed. Akira didn't like Sid's newfound enthusiasm.

"Take a seat. I was just going over what we hope to accomplish in this club. Although I've always thought 'club' sounded a little lame. So, we've been discussing a new name." A kid in the front row turned towards the back of the class. He moved the bridge of his glasses up on his head with the palm of his hand. "I suggested we call it REC. Short for Robotic Engineering Club." Sid rolled his eyes.

"Anyway," he began. "We will be competing in various tournaments. There will be individual bot competitions and group matches. Extracurricular activities…"

Akira turned to Lauren. "So what do you think?" He asked in a low whisper.

"Of Sid or the club? Because I'm pretty interested in both!" Lauren replied with a smile. She was still looking at Sid, who was still speaking to the class, when he looked at her and returned her smile. "So does anyone have any questions before I go on?" No one did, so he did go on. And on, and on, annnnnnd on. He talked about how he was a decorated Lacrosse player; what the former president of the class was like and how he intends to honor him by surpassing him and so on. Akira sat patiently throughout the whole incessant speech given by the manly and smart Sid Meyers.

At the end the two politely said their "nice to meet you"s while Lauren and Sid hugged goodbye. To Akira's dismay, when he looked back Sid was leaning against the wall by the classroom door checking out Lauren as she walked away with Akira. When Sid saw Akira look back, he gave him a wink and made his hand into a finger gun. He mouthed the word "bang" and fired the pretend gun. Akira flicked his head forward. *Hmph.*

CHAPTER 14

DREAM ENTRY 15: AFTER THE last dream entry where I was interrupted, I spent some time avoiding the use of my powers. I haven't made any leeway in figuring out who the trespasser was. Between you and I, or between just me and me, I should say perhaps; I've been honest to god terrified to "experiment" with any more powers until I either: A- figure out who the stranger is since they clearly already know who I am, or B- figure out how to cover up or hide the apparent signals that I send when I dreamwalk. I have compiled a list of possible suspects, although I still lack a motif.

Lauren-Convenient that she found me a week after someone entered my dream.. perhaps a little TOO convenient?! Maybe she's able to enter dreams without giving away her gender?

Ray-Is it possible Ray tricked me in his own head? He was the only person who was ever aware of me entering their dreams.. but why not say anything? Why even pretend to be someone else?

Corey-Playing dumb maybe? Hiding in plain sight by being very different than everyone else I've ever met? I'm watching you Corey!

Sid-Sid is a suspect because he's an arrogant jerk just like the stranger in the dream was. Unfortunately, when we both met in the dream I couldn't tell if the stranger was a pretty boy jock too.

Professor Lystrom-This teacher is always smiling at me in BIO. It's pretty creepy. It makes me feel like he knows something that I don't. Maybe he just knows my grades already.

A stranger I've yet to meet?

Entry to be continued...

• • •

"Yo dawg, that Laura girl really is a hot babe!" Corey said as he caught a baseball thrown by Ray. "How many times do we have to tell you, idiot. Her name isn't Laura." Ray said shaking his head.

"Doesn't matter anyway," Akira said. Corey threw the ball awkwardly and Akira jumped up and missed it. "She has the hots for that pretty boy I told you guys about."

"Man, I wish I could join that club with you homie, but I hate technology. Technology is for *Christians* and *actors*. If I had a choice, I wouldn't use any of it!" Corey protested. Then his phone rang and he pulled it out of his pocket to answer the text.

Akira smiled. *People at college sure are weird.* They threw the ball around until they had to part ways to get to their individual classes. When Akira went to his class and sat down at his desk, he realized he had a new text.

It was from Ray, asking him if he wanted to come to a party tonight. *I guess he didn't want to invite me in front of Corey then..* "We'll see!" he responded, and put his phone away. Another thing he noticed in college was the utter contempt professors had for kids with phones out.

It was the most fascinating thing. Seeing the faces of boys and girls he only knew through school, without actually knowing any of them. Most were quiet in class. Now Akira was seeing the inebriated versions of these people. In some cases, he thought he was seeing the "real" them. There was a girl that sat in the front of his History class doing a bump of coke. Ray made a joke about how he always knew there was a reason she liked to sit at the "front of the line" or something like that.

Another kid was always known to fall asleep during class. Without fail, he always passed out during a lecture. Akira thought he saw him fall asleep during a test too. Akira would have believed it if someone told him he was narcoleptic, but here was that same kid doing a keg stand and energetically saying hi to everyone he knew.

Imagine these kids showed the same enthusiasm in school? Then Akira brushed that thought off bashfully. *Wow, maybe I am a big nerd.*

Akira took another sip of his Bud Light. *A simple drink, for a simple guy.*

Lauren entered the room where he was people watching.

"So AK-47, you down for some beer pong?" she asked in a taunting manner.

"Oh man, I mean, I was the king back on Long Island. Let's do it. And don't call me that!" he chuckled.

"I see...perhaps the mighty King AK-47 could teach a simple girl like me a thing or two about this male dominated game?"

Laughing, Akira gave her a playful shove and followed her to where the games were going on.

In the middle of the intense toe to toe beer pong match, Akira and Lauren's opponents decided to take a break and go smoke cigarettes.

"That's a nasty habit," Lauren said.

"What, smoking cigarettes, or us winning?"

"Us winning is more of a triumphant victory that will be celebrated throughout the land!"

"Haha, oh yeah?" Looking at Lauren now made Akira feel warm. She was beautiful and charismatic. She had wit and charm. So Akira decided to take a shot in the dark.

"Would you wanna go out for something to eat sometime? Ya know, just you and me?"

She gave him a serious look, and he watched her consider it. These few seconds felt like a millennia to him. She relocated her gaze unto his. "Sure thing, it sounds like it'll be fun." Lauren smiled. Akira tried to play it cool. "Oh-okay. Awesome. Looking forward to it!"

Then the cigarette smoking duo returned to try to finish off the last three cups. Their opponents, perhaps freshly energized from nicotine now engaged in the comeback of a century. They tied the game up in only two turns.

"Wow, I didn't see that coming," Akira said in a half shrug. He was hoping to bond with Lauren over a trivial beer pong victory. His tipsy mind was focused on the all-important "we won hug". When Akira stumbled back from the bathroom a few minutes later he came back just in time to watch his defeat. Akira smoothly changed his plans, and instead he gave Lauren a "well we tried our best" embrace. Ejected off the table, Akira and Lauren went to go mingle. "I have to go to the bathroom, I'll be back in a few!" Lauren said already turning to go.

"Sure thing! I'm going to find Ray."

Akira wanted to know why Ray didn't want to invite Corey. And he wanted to know how Ray expected to keep it a secret when they all live together. Despite himself, Akira got caught up in something known as Intoxicated ADD. He became distracted by a girl in one of his classes who began talking to him about the pain in the ass teacher they shared. Ray pushed his way over to the crowded room filled with people wobbling like plants in the wind. He nodded for Akira to come over, and he said his goodbyes to the girl. "What's up!" Akira said while unconsciously tilting his body forward. Akira was thinking mostly of nachos and cheese.

"Not much amigo, but I just saw Lauren and that pretty boy go up to a room." Without realizing it, Akira straightened up, all thoughts of nachos gone. All of his intoxicated cognitive function was focused on one thing now.

"Si-Sid?".

"Yeah, that's him."

Akira suddenly looked down, and sadness washed over his face.

Ray offered a cheerful smile and scratched the back of his head.

"Wanna play a prank on them or something?"

Akira shook his head. "Nah don't worry about it. It's all good. Everything is okay! I'll be right back."

"Sure thing my man." Ray replied. He grabbed the cigarette hanging from his ear and went to go to the designated smoking area-anywhere outside.

Akira sat down. For reasons he couldn't explain he debated going to the room and walking in. *What if they're just talking. What if they're in the middle of banging? What if-* he decided he didn't want to find out. He didn't want to be at a party anymore. He just wanted to go to his bed, and wither away in privacy.

• • •

Akira sat with his legs hanging off the bed. He wished he could talk to his mom. He wished he could see her, feel her arms around him telling him everything will be okay, just as she had done throughout his life. She would always tell him how handsome he was, how much he deserved someone who would treat him right. Then reflecting on his mother hurt too much, so he thought about how Lauren said yes to him and went upstairs with Sid. Thinking about Lauren only made him begin thinking about how much he missed Amy. He felt so alone. He debated trying to call Cody or Jake, but it was 1 AM on Friday night. He didn't want to bother them or interrupt whatever fun they might be having or wake them from any slumber they might be enjoying. His problems weren't worth that to him. Especially because deep down, he knew they couldn't change anything, only he could. *Easier said than done though. I may not be able to see my mom, but I can see the woman I love the second most in the world. I'd rather see her and be miserable than be miserable and alone. Alone. I'm all alone. All alone with my self-pity and thoughts. Without Amy I am incomplete. I'm all al-*Akira fell asleep and fell onto his pillow, body half off the bed.

Akira's energy exploded. Not in the manner of a conventional explosion, but an invisible, intangible shockwave that goes completely undetected..unless you have the ability to recognize this energy. Eleven minutes after Akira fell asleep, Amelia Hernandez fell asleep beside her boyfriend Jack in her bed approximately 66.8 miles away. Five minutes after she fell asleep, she felt a familiar presence. She was in a Starbucks, her favorite place. "Akira..." she whispered.

"I'm surprised you remembered my name." Akira said harshly. He materialized in the booth next to her table. She turned her head as he spoke. As usual in his post-breakup state, he felt queasy seeing how gorgeous she was.

"Of course I do," she said, clearly offended. "I could *never* forget you." She placed special emphasis on that "n" word.

"Then why do you *always* kick me out of your life?" He asked while looking at her, watching the memories they shared playback in the reflection of her brown eyes.

Amy began twirling her hair nervously. "It's not fair to Jack. I can't help but be drawn to him. I don't know why. Every time I have to cut contact with you a part of me dies, but I do as I must. I wish I had more control of my feelings."

"Me too," he agreed, without clarifying if he was referring to himself or her.

He got up and walked behind her. She still faced forward. He began playing with her hair the way she liked. He brushed a soft hand across her cheek. Then she pushed his hand away and stood up. "Why must you torture me like this?" Amy exclaimed, almost panting.

"You sure are one to talk. Do you have any idea about what I went through? What I still go through? Every morning. Every night. Every moment of every fucking day?"

"Akira I can only imagine,"

"Every night I want you to know every wonderful thing I've done, every terrible thing I've seen. I want you to see, to understand every horrible thing I've done. Every beautiful thing I have seen. My heart is in a medieval torture device, and the pain just doesn't stop. It's like burying a pet in the backyard, I throw some dirt on top and hope to move on but those bones are always back there, even as the flesh rots away."

He watched her eyes become glassy. He had so much more to say, but he came up blank. His world was spinning again. Unreality washed over him.

"You should have been there when I needed you."

Tears began streaming down her face. Witnessing such a perfect face weep made his tears mirror hers. She began shaking her head left to right. "Why can't you say anything Amy?" *If this is just a dream, why the fuck does it feel so real?* She thought, tossing the idea back and forth in her head. Going over the words he was saying. Swallowing them one by one.

"Why can't you say anything back to that?" he repeated.

They stood there in a coffee shop filled with shadowy faces. Then unexpectedly, in Amy's version Akira disappeared instantaneously. In Akira's version, Amy vanished. However, in Akira's version. He was no longer the only dreamwalker.

Amy slumped back into her seat. She drank some of her coffee but it tasted stale. She woke up several moments later with moist cheeks. Her eyeliner ran down her face like rivers blackened from pollution. She looked at Jack and put her arms around him and held him tighter.

CHAPTER 15

EVERYTHING WENT BLACK. AGAIN. AKIRA blinked again and his eyes adjusted to the new background surrounding him. It was a beautiful meadow. The grey coffee shop was gone. "Who did that?" he called out.

Before she spoke, Akira somehow knew she was behind him, almost sensing her presence. Or her power. He was too inexperienced to tell.

She wore long dark brown hair. Even tied up in what Akira assumed was a bun, it hung past her shoulders. She spoke with a cool, experienced tone. Akira estimated she was about five years older than him. "My name is Kristen, it's nice to meet you."

"What happened to Amy?" Akira said, wiping the tears from his eyes.

Kristen gave him a sympathetic look. "I severed whatever connection you had. I'm sorry. There was no way of knowing how important or crucial the conversation was, I could only sense that you put a lot of energy into maintaining it."

Don't those both kinda mean the same thing? he thought spitefully. She walked casually around him. "I sensed she wasn't local, probably out on eastern Long Island."

"How do you know that? You obviously have dreamwalking powers like me. In fact, if I'm being perfectly honest, I was warned about you, I think."

Although she wasn't facing Akira, she smiled at the phrase dreamwalking. *It's always interesting hearing what they come up with.* She was watching a sunrise over the meadow. It was illuminating daisies and six-foot-tall sunflowers alike. There was a plethora of flowers of all different kinds in the distance. She loved to do her work in beautiful places. It was definitely a benefit being able to dream up whatever you want. She decided to get back on track.

"Warned of me? That's quite unlikely. Unless..hmm. Interesting." She put a finger to her mouth. Akira turned to face her back. He saw her red nail polish matched her red lipstick. She was beautiful. Although, *to me, no one is more beautiful than Amy,* Akira thought sadly.

"Unless what?"

She turned and smiled at him, although in the smile Akira thought he saw that something wasn't right.

"It's not important right now."

Interrupting her, he shouted "Well then what is?!"

"You have a gift. This could be used in good or bad ways. The organization of which I'm a part of, keeps people with this gift safe and keeps regular people safe from us. Even if they don't know it. I want to meet you in person. I've spent several weeks trying to track down your location and find out more about you. Please consider our offer, and we will train you to use your powers to their fullest, along with morally sound applications for it. I will enter your memory and leave information there for tomorrow. When you wake up, you will know where to go if you so desire."

"And if I refuse? What if I don't want you going through my memories?" Akira asked.

"They always say that," she said almost to herself. "And the answer is always the same. Then someone in our organization will be forced to keep a tab on you at all times. If you don't mind someone following you, watching you, and monitoring all your dreams and what not, then I guess it's not that big of a deal." Sighing, she met his eyes. "And if you don't want me to access your memories, that's just too bad. Unless you decide to train with us, then you can learn how to block someone out. Anyways, don't worry. I'm not going to pry, I'm just gonna leave the directions to the meeting. Should you choose to come of course."

Thinking everything over made Akira feel a little light headed.

"What's the name of the organization you work for?"

"We go by a simple acronym. M-L-K. Think it over."

Before Akira could reply he woke up instantly. *I guess she "cut our connection"*. Lying there watching the ceiling, Akira tried to re-member every single detail he could. He turned on his phone and google searched MLK. Everything that popped up had to do with Martin Luther King Junior. Akira tried sifting through less popu-lar results but came across more of the same.

"Hey man, you're up."

Akira jumped and hid his phone without even thinking about it. It was Corey, and he was sitting there with a blank expression on his face.

"Jesus dude! You damn near scared the piss out of me!" Akira said while turning off his phone's screen.

"Sorry man. Did you wake up just to look at some porn?" Corey asked casually.

"Wh-what? No man. Not at all."

"It's okay home fry, I've been there. When you're sad about someone you love or used to love, you'll do anything to get your mind off them. Sometimes thinking about naked strangers is bet-ter than remembering good times with the person you loved. It's certainly easier."

Akira was uncomfortable with the topic. Then he realized, "Wait, what makes you think I'm sad?"

"Well AK-47, you were into that Lori girl and all of her snapchat story is her and that guy you don't like making out and taking pic-tures together." Corey said dryly.

"Actually I forgot all about that...good for them."

"Oh, sorry to bring it up then AK."

Akira was suddenly filled with shame when he comprehended that Corey saw a bunch of videos on social media of a party that he wasn't invited to.

"So what did you do tonight Corey?"

Noticeably embarrassed, Corey turned his head away as if he had been slapped.

"Not much my bro, I mostly just went for a walk. Went and bought a couple of dutches to smoke with."

Addressing the elephant in the room, Akira said "Well, I wish you could have came tonight. You're a cool guy C-dawg." He found that he meant it too.

Corey smiled and then let out a heartwarming laugh.

"C-dawg. I like it!"

"Of course you do!" Akira teased.

They talked for another hour about life. Akira told Corey more about Amy. Corey revealed that he was actually bisexual. The last person that hurt him was a guy named Larry. Akira accepted his friend, but felt sad that he was so ashamed of his sexuality. *It's 2020 god damnit, and people still feel like this* he thought. Their conversation continued into a discourse on true love, true pain, and coping with these human emotions. At 3:43 AM Ray returned to the dorm room and the duo decided to pretend to be asleep. Then Akira remembered what he had to do tomorrow. He decided it was time to go to sleep for real. He drifted into dreamless slumber.

CHAPTER 16

TOSSING A 5-HOUR ENERGY DRINK into the garbage, Dmitri retired to the bed he was renting. It was pitiful. He sensed many things had occurred here that he wished to avoid learning about more intricately. "Ignorance is bliss szoh zhey say." he said through a heavy accent. One can only Americanize so much. There almost always will be hints of an immigrant's true home. For Dmitri, it was the remnants of his Russian accent. Dmitri knew he made the right choice by staying up all night. Now, he knew where his prey was hiding. The boy had worked perfectly as bait.

Dmitri decided it was time to sleep. With powers of his magnitude, he could go days without sleeping and still function at a peak level. Of course this was also because whenever he dream shifted, his evil energy sucked the victim dry of all the energy stored in sleep and during REM. Victims who he dream shifted into woke up more fatigued than ever, and on some occasions if he so desired, did not wake up at all.

Sitting on the couch, he closed his eyes. "Zee couch weel do fyne." Dmitri said, throwing a blanket he brought with him over his legs. All of his hard work was paying off, now it was time to rest, not meditate. Deep sleep for the first time all week was almost exciting.

• • •

Akira woke up feeling what he could only describe as fresh. It was 8 AM, which would mean that he got only about four hours of sleep. The realization of the fresh sensation was only the second thing he acknowledged as he awoke; the first being the location of his meeting with Kristen. He had to take a train back towards Long Island and then get off at the Woodside exit. From there he would look for the train car designated **7566**. The MLK left this message almost like a voicemail in his head. He knew they would deal with the workers at the station. He wasn't entirely sure how, but he knew he would be effectively invisible to them.

With all of this knowledge, Akira jumped out of bed and grabbed a notebook. He copied everything down incase his memory faded. Akira was assaulting a notebook with his pen when he remembered the time. On a weekday it wasn't really *that* early. But everyone in college knows 8 AM on a Saturday morning is earlier than any other day. Unsurprisingly, Corey and Ray were still sleeping. Ray was engulfed in blankets beyond visibility, and Corey was snoring. Looking at the two, Akira wondered if Ray was homophobic. He certainly hoped not, but some ignorant ideas of the human race were near impossible to kill off entirely.

With haste, Akira filled a backpack with items he always brought on adventures and he rushed out the door. He'd have to catch the exact train Kristen wanted out of Penn. Good thing he was feeling refreshed.

. . .

Lucas Dubois was happy his parents gave him so much freedom. Being an honor student back in France, his parents thought him very capable of handling himself. Some might even say they underestimated the dangers of New York City. Others might say they permitted their fourteen-year-old son too much freedom. Lucas would say that they should have lent him more money.

He wandered around the various stores, laughed at the crudely created costumes of cartoon characters begging to take pictures with people's kids for cash. He stopped laughing when he saw how much money they were charging people. Was it pity? Appeasement to their kids? Lucas himself only wanted a four-foot-tall model of an AT-AT walker from Star Wars. Unfortunately, it cost more than the money his parents lent him. He suspected they didn't know the transfer rate between Euros and dumb American dollars.

Mouth agape, he stared at the picture of the model walker in the window of the toy store. Drool might have come from his mouth, or he might have just imagined that.

"That things pretty damn cool," said a stranger from behind him.

"You don't even know the half of it." Lucas said, thinking about how the model could fit action figures in the pilot area and the belly. Everything was to scale and a perfect replica from the ones in the movies Lucas grew up loving.

Then it dawned on him that the stranger wasn't a passerby, but in fact standing right behind him. Without looking, he turned and began power walking down the road. The man kept his pace, or so Lucas thought he heard. He craned his neck to look, and when he did the man reached out and grabbed his wrist. "Hey! What are you doing?" Lucas yelled out.

The man immediately released his grip but had an interesting look in his eyes. "Hey kid, just hear me out." The stranger with a goatee and a beanie pleaded.

"What are you some kind of pedophile? I don't want *anything* that much. Not even a hundred AT-ATs." Lucas stood there reluctantly, but kept checking the perimeter constantly to make sure someone was walking on the street.

"Not even a hundred and one of those? I'll get you an AT-AT or whatever it is, if you help me raise money. See, I've got to get on a train, but I'll get thrown off and maybe even arrested if I can't afford a ticket. I've spent too much money on my way to New York. You're a kid, just, uh, I don't know, pretend you're poor or something and I'm sure people will donate some money."

The man watched as Lucas thought it over. "But if you don't have money, how would you get me the model?"

"If we make enough, you can keep all of it minus my train ticket. If we don't, you can still keep that much, and I'll steal one. Yes, I'll break a law to keep a promise, yessir indeedy." Lucas watched the stranger place his hand on his forehead and squeeze his eyes shut with great curiosity. *Well. I guess I can always outrun this weirdo if he does try anything. He does seem like he needs some help pretty bad.*

• • •

His mind flashed back to a time when he was but a boy. He was only twelve. Not much younger than the child in front of him.

"Daddy, can I have a Darth Vader?"

"Of course you can son, just don't tell your brother. Kenneth just got expelled and we won't reward that one bit."

The memory was still crisp and fresh. It brought tears to his eyes that he immediately wiped away.

The boy seemed resourceful enough to Philip. He admired how cautious the boy was. Philip Anthony Stone always appreciated intelligence. Or rather the voice inside his head who called himself Kenneth appreciated intelligence. Kenneth cared more about the mission they were given by the being they came to know only as the Dark Voice. This Dark Voice invaded their dreams and collectively scared the shit out of both of them. A few times he was even more than a voice, he was a Dark Man. Seeing his physical form was like seeing an atom bomb up close. A faint sense that it would be cold and metallic to the touch, but a lingering sense of danger and the explosive capabilities. Cold, murderous intent completely void of regret.

Philip peered around the corner of an alleyway he was hiding in. He saw the boy called Lucas dancing. A few people were there watching him with sympathetic faces, but most ignored him. Philip figured that they believed if they did not look directly at the boy, they couldn't be held responsible for keeping their money to themselves. Philip actually saw a man and woman glare judgmentally at the boy. He didn't know why they threw such angry and snobby looks at him, but it made his blood boil. It took Kenneth to remind him he couldn't make an incident. Then Philip saw an old lady talking to Lucas. Philip decided it was best to get a closer look. Upon closer inspection, he realized the old lady was trying to abduct the boy. Or save him, by her standards.

"You've got to come with me, thisn't no place for a boy your age. Where's your parents?" she asked in a reprimanding tone, as if she were his grandmother.

"Look lady, it's fine I just need money for a meal. My parents are okay." Lucas said, still dancing. His clothes were dirty from being on the ground during break dancing bits. It made his act that much more believable.

"I'm going to get an officer of the law to help you sonny. I'll be right back."

The old lady sped past the alleyway Philip was in seconds later with her walker, clearly intent on doing something good today.

Philip and Lucas relocated before she could return. Amazingly in under an hour, Lucas had acquired $23.50.

"I'll be right back kid, don't go anywhere." Philip said turning and walking back the way they came.

"Now you sound like that old geezer!" Lucas called out jokingly. Phil's walk became a slow jog, then a run.

After fifteen minutes of continued dancing and joke telling to raise money, Lucas wondered if Philip was ever going to come back. He only held onto a five, and a few ones. Lucas had the rest of the money. But was that enough for him to abandon the kid and go on the train?

"Man, screw that guy." Lucas declared after twenty minutes passed. He took out the cell phone he was concealing and began to dial his parents' phone number.

"Um, excuse me, are you the kid that was dancing for money?"

Lucas looked up and saw another kid maybe a year or two older than him. He was carrying a large paper bag. "Maybe I was, what of it?"

"This smelly bearded man gave me half a pack of cigarettes to bring this around the block to you. It looks like it's worth more than these ciggs so you better take it quick before I change my mind."

Lucas reluctantly took the bag from the other kid. He couldn't really speak, so he smiled and nodded at the other boy who nodded back and disappeared back into the New York City streets. The AT-AT walker was still in a box and everything. It more than made up for the undeniable explanation he'd have to create to explain to his parents how he got so dirty. Lucas suddenly had a weird thought. He kind of wish he asked that guy what his name was. He wished him well and went to find his parents.

• • •

You shouldn't have wasted time getting that kid the stupid toy. Don't you see how close of a call this was? Worse, if we got caught grabbing that, we'd be fried. Done for. Finito amigo. The train door slid shut right behind him as the conductor's voice resonated throughout the station. "This is the train to Ronkonkoma."

Philip couldn't afford to take a seat. He had been instructed to find an Asian boy. During a nightmare the night before, Philip was surrounded by people whose faces all melted into that of the boy. With the image burned into his brain, he began walking down the aisle. "If you do something for someone, you should be rewarded. He paid for this train ticket, and we're here now." Philip said out loud to himself. Several people watched him talk to himself as he walked down the aisle, but most New Yorker's are quite desensitized to people talking to themselves. Especially on a train.

Walking into the next train car, Philip continued his search diligently, occasionally stopping to glance more carefully at Asian passengers that looked similar. *Don't forget to be subtle. He told us to neutralize the boy after we found out where to go to find the rest.* "Yeah yeah yeah yeah! I know." *Look over there? That one with the headphones. What do you think?* Without answering out loud Philip knew he found his target. Soon the nightmares would be gone and Philip Anthony Stone could start life completely fresh. A new stake in things. There wasn't a whole lot he wouldn't do for another chance.

Akira sat in a two-person seat by himself reading a book, occasionally shooting a glance out the window to look at the passing scenery. There wasn't much to look at this close to the city, Akira thought. Sometimes he'd look the other way to make sure a conductor wasn't coming to collect his ticket. A lot of people complained about taking trains, but Akira actually didn't mind it all that much. It was better than a bus or a taxi. The only bad thing was that train stations were always in bad areas. *One more exit to go. I don't know what to expect, but I can't wait.* The excitement flooded his brain, making it hard to concentrate on reading. Akira put the book back in his backpack. He began to wonder how Cody and Jake were again. He decided he'd call their parents and check in and see how everyone was. "This is the train to Ronkonkoma. This station is…"

"…Woodside. The next station is Jamaica." Getting up, the boy made sure he had everything with him. Taking in a noticeable amount of breath before sighing, the kid prepared himself. Philip got up and went to the other exit in the train car. Walking out into the open environment and getting blasted by freezing weather, he placed his hood up. The workers were paying no mind to Akira or Philip. Only one other worker exited the train. The oriental boy got off the train platform and walked into a building. Walking past the workers shuffling about their duties, he acted as if he owned the place. Philip tried to replicate this as he followed several feet behind. If he followed any further, he could potentially lose him. Philip was decently sure his footsteps were being masked by whatever music the kid was listening to anyway.

Akira stood staring at a doorway. It read: **Employees Only!** But he knew deep in his subconscious that this was the route picked out for him. Like Kristen had said, all of the workers at the station ignored his presence. He wasn't sure how, but he seemed invisible to them. If it weren't for that, Akira might think they were in on this MLK business too or whatever. Maybe they still were. *Welp, I might as well begin my trespassing now. Time's-a-wastin.* Akira pushed the door open and walked through. There was a long hallway. Two doors. One door said: **Operations** and the other read: **Do not**

enter. The latter had an actual padlock on it. "Oh what the hell," Akira said as he glanced from door to door. Then he simply knew that there was a key hidden in the exit sign above the door he just entered from. He climbed onto a bench that stuck out from the wall and he was high enough to take off the EXIT sign. Grabbing the key, he returned to the padlock and unlocked it. He put the key back in the exit sign. After entering the "Do not enter" door, he closed the padlock and let the door shut behind him. As he audibly heard the door close behind him, he realized that he locked himself in. Fear washed over him briefly.

There was a staircase ahead. Descending the staircase, Akira realized he walked down approximately three floors worth of stairs. At the end there was a wooden door. Grabbing the knob and expecting it to be locked, his hand turned the knob and the door opened. Yet *another passageway*. Akira half-knew that this was where his implanted memory came to an end. This had to be it. But interestingly enough, there was a paper taped to the door at the end. Akira moved closer to read. Expecting it to be some sort of rules, he took out his headphones and put his iPod in his pocket. The sign read:

> **Walk through this door and then run. Take this paper with you and go to the Fairfield Inn nearest this station.**

Confused and kind of pissed off, Akira complied. He tore the note off and stuffed it into his pocket. He opened the door. And that's when he heard someone descend the last step to the staircase behind him.

CHAPTER 17

SO IT WAS ALL ONE big, wild goose chase? Akira wasn't sure why he was sent to this strange place, but he was suddenly sure he heard someone's footsteps behind him. As he turned, time seemed to slow down until it was dripping by. He saw a figure practically leap off of the last step and lunge in his direction. Immediately recognizing the man to be an adult, Akira grabbed the paper note and backed himself out the doorway and slammed the door. Just as he did so, the full force of the man hit the doorway. It made a loud bang, but the door stood firm. Akira locked the door as fast he could. He took a fresh breath of air. He knew that lock wouldn't hold someone that determined for long.

Akira burst through a door that led into a warehouse. It seemed to be an outdated storage facility. It was dark except for some tainted light seeping in from a rectangular window. Akira didn't know if he should search for a weapon, or a way out. Then he heard the door break open. He ran and stumbled over an old wrench, but he caught his balance. The stranger was gaining on him. But Akira was faster. The stalker picked up the wrench Akira tripped on mid-run and chucked it as hard as he could. It hit a crate in front of Akira. He flinched as the crate exploded in a tornado of splinters. Then he rounded a corner, and caught his breath. He could tell the man wasn't running anymore. Looking around,

Akira solemnly realized there were no doors in the room other than the one he came in. He quietly climbed up a crate he was leaning against. The same second he glanced back to check his six, his leg was grabbed. Akira was torn off and fell a good six feet to the ground. It hurt.

"Who the hell are-" the man punched Akira in the face. He went to punch again but Akira blocked his face. He still felt the blow in his arms though. The man kicked and Akira rolled out of the way. Akira swung his leg as hard as he could in a sweep but the man saw it coming and jumped over it. But as he landed Akira extended his leg into the stalker's crotch. He howled out in pain. Akira got up and uppercut punched him. But it barely even moved his chin, so then Akira leaned forward and pushed him as hard as he could knocking him over. Akira went to run back the way he came, but the man climbed a crate and took a shortcut through them. Jumping, he caught up with Akira and slammed his face into the unforgiving floor in a tackle. Pinned on top of Akira, the man triumphantly exhaled a deep breath before collecting himself.

"Who were you meeting with and where?" The man asked.

"I don't know what you're talking about. I got lost." The man leaned all his weight on his knee. The knee dug into Akira's back, where he audibly groaned in pain. In fact, he wanted to scream, but he didn't want to give the psycho the satisfaction. Not like anyone would hear him down here anyway.

"I know he's lying, but he seems awfully content on keeping the lie."

The psycho sounded like he was talking to an accomplice that (hopefully) wasn't there.

Akira was staring at a pile of crates. If there was just some way he could crash into that pile, it would all come falling down. He might be able to flee this psycho after an erratic move like that.

The pain in his back was only getting worse. He felt like his spine was going to snap at any moment. Akira also became aware that he bit his lip when his face smashed into the ground. He spat out blood onto the ground next to him.

The man took his arms off of Akira's to reach into his pockets. Akira stretched his neck painfully to see what the man was getting. Out of a small pack, the man grabbed rope. *Holy shit--holy shit. It's now, or never.* Using both his hands and all of his pinned down weight, he pushed himself to one side. The assailant lost some balance because the skinny body he was holding himself up on with his knee suddenly jerked away. While his arms wobbled as he tried to balance himself, Akira turned over now on his back and kicked with both his feet. The impact hit the man directly in the stomach sending him backwards. He hit his head on the ground when he fell. Akira turned for the doorway. Then he saw the disoriented man still lying down holding his head. Akira ran around and pushed the tower of crates forward. The wooden mountain landed on his attacker. Akira left the room and heard the loud sounds of the crates crashing down in an avalanche, then the wood splintering and dispersing everywhere.

Akira wasted no time exiting the station as fast as he could. On the way out he wondered if it was possible he even killed the man. He considered calling the cops and mentioning how he chased him. Akira took out his phone as he stepped outside the last door blocking his way to the outside station. It brandished a new crack in the screen. Akira also took out the note. Trying to type in the walking directions to the Fairfield Inn was more difficult than it should have been because he was still shaking.

• • •

Akira was looking for any sign. Was he going to meet a secret agent? Is he supposed to pick a specific room? The vagueness was killing him. The note didn't even specify how long he should stay at this inn. He walked around his room in circles. He watched TV. He started charging his phone and playing games on it. Anything to pass the time. Anything to distract his mind. He got up at one point, and went to the door, fully prepared to just go back to college and pretend none of this ever happened. He stood with with his hand on the knob for several moments. Akira ultimately decided that he needed to stay in that room until something happened. He just hoped that bearded man didn't burst through the door. And he hoped he wasn't making a mistake by not involving the police.

• • •

Kristen Pierce was in a meditative position on a hotel bed when she sensed it. *The boy has finally fallen asleep.* She opened her eyes, and uncrossed her legs. Taking out her cell phone, she dialed a number quickly.

"Hello Sniper. What's the update?" The voice was calmer than usual in this type of situation. Kristen could never tell if he just wanted her to think that he resonated serenity, or if the situation really was good.

"Well, Kilimanjaro, the boy just fell asleep in the inn we instructed him to go to. It looks like he survived the trap you set for him. I hope you know how much I disapprove. I'm going to commence with the operation after this conversation."

"Excellent," he said, ignoring her disapproval. He certainly sounded pleased. "Don't forget that this is just reconnaissance though, be careful that you remain undetected. Don't forget we needed to test the boy's resilience and confirm that someone was following him. Report to me after you're done. I'll be up."

These missions never are cakewalks, are they?

"Copy that. Sniper out."

• • •

The first thing Akira remembered was talking to his mom. They were having a normal conversation in the kitchen. Then she brought up Amy. Normally Akira's smile would have dissipated, his heart would of skipped a beat and he would have fought back sad thoughts. But this time he answered as if nothing had happened.

Akira felt like he was watching this transpire from outside of his body. Then the Akira he was watching talk to his dead mother said the unspeakable. "You know that I miss you and wish you were alive every single day right?"

He thought his mom would cry. He wanted to cry, but he couldn't.

"Yes, honey I know. I love you and wish I could come back too." But she answered with a smile, rather than sadness. Akira was confused, so confused. Then a very audible gust of wind started blowing outside the house. The windows blew in, shattering glass. The front door smacked open. Akira finally lost control of himself, and his eyes started watering. He turned around and his mom was gone.

"Mom, where did you go? MOOOOM?" He called out not caring how loud it sounded, how childish it felt, how needy, how weak and helpless doing it made him feel.

"Your mutter iz gone, boy. And she izn't coming back." A deep voice boomed, echoing throughout Akira's old apartment as if there was a loud speaker blasting the voice.

"Who said that? Who are you and what do you want with me?"

Akira only semi-consciously realized he was shaking again. It was also the first time Akira could ever remember feeling this cold in a dream. The windows and door might have been opened, sure, but it was still a dream wasn't it? Then in the doorway was a darkened figure, not totally unlike the one that entered his dreams the other time but Akira immediately knew it was a completely different person.

This figure's hood was not merely black, but it was a hood of some sort of evil energy. It sizzled and sparked. The hood and the cloak were very much as alive as the thing wearing them. Akira saw red eyes glow in the hood. The cloaked thing-not man anymore, of that Akira was sure, reached his hand out. Akira began lifting off of the floor. Then he felt invisible fingers wrap around his neck. His first thought was *Holy shit, what's happening to me?* Then *Wow this is kind of like Star Wars,* and then the realization that he couldn't breathe. As he began asphyxiating, he was calming himself down. *Don't worry, it's just a dream, if you die, you'll just wake up. IT'S OKAY. It'll be okay.*

The cloaked monster that was levitating him three feet off the ground and choking him began laughing. It was a hysteric, maniacal laugh. Then collecting himself, the darkened being said "Don't worry, dying in your dream may not exactly kill you, but it will surrender your will to me. You'll be comatose soon, just like your dear mutter was. And then after that, your pain will be gone."

Life is a constant battle between good and evil. His mom had said that. Akira guessed she had been right.

The evil laughter continued where it left off. Yes, Akira decided it was definitely an evil force that was laughing. He thought over the dark implications of what the humanoid monster just implied. Now Akira was being choked against the wall of his apartment, still inches off of the floor. He struggled to keep his eyes open. The last thing he was thinking about was the hatred and pity he felt deep in his heart. *My life has been a waste.* Then darkness engulfed him.

There will always be choices, and there will always be decisions.

I know my son will make the right ones.

CHAPTER 18

AKIRA WAS LAYING AGAINST THE wall of his apartment. He was a crumpled mess; a discarded beer can. He was wondering when he would simply pass on and his miserable life would be forgotten. He failed to register the fact that he fell from the telekinetic suspension after an explosion rocked the apartment. Then his blurred vision dissipated and he saw a flaming crater where his roof should have been. Akira coughed and some blood and phlegm shot out onto his carpet. The smell of fire invaded his nostrils. Another explosion shook his entire world. "Why can't I wake up... what's going on?" He asked no one in particular.

Akira felt like he was drowning. He thought of his mom. His *mommy*. His love, Amy. *Oh god how it hurts. Someone else goes inside of you and then sleeps beside you and confides within you. For some reason, him calling your name is worse than any imagery of him plowing you. It's a name that's always on the tip of my tongue, ready to roll off, but never quite ready to leave. Oh god, am I going to die here?*

We should talk to our emotions. Confront them head on.

Akira used his vivid imagination to picture a clone of himself standing up looking down at him. Despite consciously creating this doppelganger, he asked: "Who are you?"

"I am Despair," the mirror image of himself replied. It wasn't a mirror image anymore. It was Akira the day after his mom died.

When he found Amy had moved on from him. The clone kept shifting. Different hair lengths, muscle sizes, outfits, different Akiras from different times of pain. "I am all of your fears fused into one. You're scared. You have been for some time now."

"Well, I'm only human."

"You're not going to make it out of here. Are you prepared to exist as a vegetable? It's alright. The outside world has nothing but sour intentions. It wishes to harm us."

"No," the Akira leaning against the wall said matter-of-factly. His face represented his calm demeanor. "There is too much that I have to do. One day I will have a kid and be an amazing parent just like my Mom. I want to fall in love and not have to worry. About anything. To fall asleep at night and not have to wonder if she'll still love me tomorrow. Maybe I'll even have two kids."

"You're naive."

"No, you are. I know life hits hard, but I will keep moving forward. For my mom. For my friends. For the MLK. For *myself.* End of story."

The doppelganger vanished. Akira's Despair faded away.

Getting up, he stumbled to the front door. He was still quite dazed and disoriented.

As he opened the door, he couldn't believe what he saw. The dark figure that choked him out like he was some kind of cheap hooker was staring down what looked like a Saturday morning cartoon come to life. It must have been about fourteen feet tall Akira decided. It was a giant robot with a red and blue paintjob. Akira was unsure if he should laugh or faint.

Out of nowhere, a jetpack appeared on the robot's back. Akira could hear gears turning and interior machinations at work. Fire shot out of the jetpack, literally cooking the ground beneath it, then after a second, the robot took off. Shooting up into the sky, it fired rockets that appeared on its shoulders at the dark figure. Flames danced on the ground where it jettisoned from. The Dark Man held his hand out and a glass-like wall appeared out of thin air. The glass had a purplish-black color emanating from it. The missiles hit the wall and exploded, and to Akira's surprise the glass didn't shatter and implode on him. While Akira was still in a state of confusion, the robot's thrusters shut off and he began to fall back towards Earth. Then at the last possible moment, he leaned forward and they turned back on. He shot himself under the glass wall which now began to crack and disintegrate, then he went to grab the figure. The robot was about grab The Dark Man in his oversized hands. Akira realized he was silently rooting for the robot.

Then the Dark Man was swallowed by the purplish-black energy and he disappeared in an instant. The momentum caused the robot to keep flying even after he passed through where the Dark Man was only moments ago.

Akira's head turned to the Dark Man's new location once he heard a peculiar noise that sounded like an electrical shock. The Dark Man immediately fired a black beam of energy from his hand that went as fast as a bullet. Its trajectory did not stray, and it quickly caught up to the Robot who was beginning to turn around. It pierced his jetpack, and then came out the other end, exiting his chest. It seemed like the robot hung there for a while, like a shish kebab in the sky. Then it exploded.

Akira couldn't figure out if the whole robot blew up, or just the jetpack. His question was answered when a jetpack-less robot began falling from the sky, leaving behind an oval of black smoke.

"I don't know who you are, but you're definitely too untrained to be em-ale-kay. Zhis boy iz mine, and you shall suffer da consequences for interfering."

The Dark Man's voice boomed throughout the world like he was speaking into a loudspeaker. Akira couldn't bear to watch the robot fall. Only a few more feet. He wondered if it would land in a crumpled mess, or another explosion. He wondered if he would ever see his friends in the real world ever again. Cody. Jake. Coop. Angela. Ray. Corey. Even Lauren. And Amy. *My dear Amy, how I miss you so. If it was your life at risk, I'd fight every single moment I could for you, even if you didn't love me back... how did he know about my mom..?*

Then Akira was snapped back to unreality when the robot's descent was slowed feet away from the ground. He saw a woman with pretty hair dressed in the opposite clothes of The Dark Man. Her clothes were all white, with a hood that complimented her beautiful face. Her dress was long, down to her ankles. It was Kristen. Her hands were sending a silver energy down to the robot, holding him in suspension until she gently put him down. "Dare are more on da way. Wunderful. Just facking great. I will still succeed, and there's nothing you wurms can do about it. Ahaha." Lightning struck the Dark Man, and he teleported, leaving a black scorch mark where he was standing.

Akira finally felt safe enough to go over to Kristen and the robot. It was weird, now he didn't just think he would be safe. He felt it too. He no longer felt the despair he did just by the Dark Man's presence.

The metal on the robot's head receded, and Akira realized it was a helmet, not a head. It also dawned on Akira that the face was that of Sid Meyers. "You've got to be goddamn kidding me."

"What's up nerd. You finally done getting choked out?"

Akira was staring in disbelief. In fact, he wouldn't have been surprised if his mouth was hanging wide open without him knowing it. Meanwhile, blood was dripping out of Sid's.

• • •

As Sid got out of his mech, it started fading away. All that was left of it after thirty seconds was a single cube and a jumpsuit. Sid grabbed the cube and put in his pocket. There was a fist sized hole in his chest, but the remainder of the mech-suit jumpsuit had begun fusing itself into his chest. Sid's face showed mild irritation and pain while the flesh healed itself.

"How the hell did you do that?"

He scoffed as if the answer was so obvious.

"Listen, I've got to go before the interrogation really begins."

"But I only asked you one question?"

"I wasn't talking about you," Sid said looking over Akira's shoulder at Kristen walking towards him.

Akira was momentarily distracted by how gorgeous she looked wearing all white.

"That was pretty impressive kid."

Akira and Sid both answered "Thanks!" simultaneously then looked at each other.

"I've already told you people I'm not joining the MLK." Sid said while staring at her. Akira suddenly remembered that all of this was because he was trying to join them.

"Well, why not kid?"

"Stop calling me that,"

"Okay child, but listen,"

"That's not much better." he said through his teeth.

"We won't force you to do anything. But if we ever find out you are misusing your powers…" she let her words hang there for a second, "then we will destroy you."

Akira swallowed hard. He wasn't sure what anyone was or wasn't capable of anymore. Even Sid looked a little frightened. He maintained her gaze, then broke it off suddenly.

"Yeah, yeah. Adios." A blue pillar of light came out of the sky and hit Sid. Akira flinched. *Oh shit, are they gonna destroy him now?* But Sid remained unscathed and started ascending the air through the blue pillar.

"That is how he stops dream shifting. The circumstances of one's powers are different depending on if they are shifting in a non-fighter's dreams, or if there are multiple active shifters. The shifter is obviously the most powerful when they are alone."

Absorbing that, Akira replied "Did you just implicate that I'm a fighter..?"

"To be completely honest, we had enough intel to believe that you were being followed. We couldn't risk our true base being found out by the agents of evil. It seemed my senses were on point again. You were followed by two individuals. I will now take you to our real base, where you will train as a real Dream Shifter."

Before Akira could respond, the outside plains in front of his apartment that only existed in his dreams vanished. He awoke back in the motel room where Kristen was sitting in a chair beside him.

"Don't look so surprised. When I severed the connection you resumed REM sleep, to dreamlessly refill the energy of your brain and soul. Now get your things."

Akira was just impressed that he wasn't dreaming anymore, because Kristen looked even more beautiful in person. He had a lot of questions still, and he was a bit angry about how coldly she treated his near death experience back at the warehouse. But he pushed such things into the back of his mind for now. "Let's do this." He said in the most confident sounding voice he could.

PART IV

THE MLK

...

CHAPTER 19

Akira was sitting in the passenger seat, quietly observing the city pass behind him. They were crossing into New Jersey, or *The Land of Smells* as Akira knew it. The windows of Kristen's large SUV were dark and tinted. "Would I be able to, well um, plug my phone charger in?" Akira asked, nervous and embarrassed to be the one interrupting the silence.

She turned and looked at him about as long as a driver could while still focusing on the road. "Sure thing kid. But you're not going to be allowed to have it on you when we get there."

"Yeah yeah yeah, no flash photography, selfies, or GPS tracking. I got it."

"Smartass," she said smiling. Akira noticed how often she looked at the rearview mirror. *Being careful is no joke to these people. Why would they want to risk everything by bringing me in?*

The entirety of the trip continued mostly in silence. Akira began feeling drowsy. It became a battle to stay awake. The cars on the six lane freeway began to blur. Akira remembered being excited to ask her questions during the trip. Now he recognized that his energy was slowly draining out of him.

".....Did....you drug me...?" Akira was struggling to keep his eyes opened.

She only smiled. His chin dropped to his chest, and then he was out.

• • •

Akira woke up in the SUV by himself. He looked around to find that he was in a large underground garage with several other bland SUVs and two-door cars. Akira began looking for his phone so he could check the time. After patting all of his pockets he realized his phone and backpack weren't in the car. As he opened the door and got out, he was almost surprised he wasn't locked in the car.

Akira analyzed the garage doors behind the line of parked cars. There was some kind of high-tech computer panel. He didn't think he was going out that way. That only left a door on the far side of the garage. It was next to a giant fridge. Behind the door was a hallway with several doors on both sides. Akira ignored them as he walked down it. At the end of the hallway there was a bunch of people talking. He was able to single out Kristen's voice, but he couldn't yet hear what they were saying. The hallway ended in a small kitchen, with a table that could only fit about three people. There were two ways out of the kitchen other than the way Akira entered. He walked to his right, guessing that was where the talking was originating.

It was a large circular room. There was a large circular table in the middle, big enough to sit about twelve people. Newspaper and magazine cutouts were scattered across the table almost like a tablecloth. A 32" flat screen TV hung in the corner of the room. It was playing local news, and after a quick glance Akira remembered he was in New Jersey.

Despite the size of the circular room, Akira only saw three people in it. He debated on trying to eavesdrop, but he took note that the man sitting down at the table was facing him. The man silently acknowledged his presence. There was a tall muscular black man, wearing a dark green beanie doing most of the talking. His back was facing Akira. As soon as Akira put one foot in the room though, he stopped talking abruptly. More loudly than before, he said: "Ah. So he's finally awake."

• • •

Kristen turned immediately. She tried to gauge if Akira was mad at her or not, or so he thought. "So you guys are the MLK?"

The black man in the beanie turned at that. "Yea. We are."

Akira now realized there was one other person in the room, a lanky looking kid around his age, with hair even longer than his. It was dyed a dark blue in the back, and his long bangs in the front were dyed a bright sky blue. He was leaning against the wall and staring at his phone, pretty much ignoring Akira's entire existence.

Akira decided to return the favor to him.

"Don't look too impressed all at once," the man with the beanie said. "You may call me Kilimanjaro."

Akira almost blurted out a laugh.

"You've already met Sniper." he said, gesturing to Kristen.

"You mean Kristen?"

He gave Akira a sour look, let it hang there, then passed it to Kristen.

"You told him your real name?"

She shrugged. "I had a feeling he'd become one of us soon, so I felt the need for our codenames were a bit.. unnecessary as far as safety measures go."

The blue haired kid glanced over his cell phone at the group.

"Yeah, Jack just likes to act tough and pretend this job is the coolest thing. It's not. You might as well just forget our names and run on home college boy." he said, before turning his attention back to his phone.

The man in the beanie, apparently Jack, walked over to the blue haired kid. He grabbed his shirt collar and jerked him off the wall. "Blizzard, how many times do I have to tell you to take things seriously?" He lifted him an inch off the ground. Blizzard's face remained uninterested, as if it wasn't his first time being lifted off of the floor by someone, or maybe this was just a daily thing for him and Jack.

Without warning, Jack spun on his heel and chucked Blizzard onto the table and his lanky body began to slide off of it from the force of the throw. Blizzard managed to grip the table while he was sliding, so when he fell off he did a backflip and landed on his feet, grinning and unperturbed. He still had his cell phone in his hand.

"You're ridiculous," Jack muttered.

"So when do I get a code name?" Akira asked earnestly.

"We don't even know if you got what it takes to be one of us yet." Jack replied.

"So how do I prove myself?"

"By getting trained. If you can survive it, and I decide that we can trust you, then you're in."

The serious facial expression Jack maintained and the way he said *survive* left a bad pit in his stomach.

"Sniper will contact you next weekend. We know you need to keep up appearances for school, but rest assured, if you succeed with us, your future will be more important than anything you could ever achieve from a formal education."

"If you say so."

"Dismissed."

Everyone began leaving the room. The blue haired kid walked past Akira and bumped shoulders with him. Then he walked towards the garage. Jack left out of the opposite door into an area Akira hadn't yet explored. He was followed by the man who sat quietly at the table the entire time. Akira noted that he looked European. He also noted that the guy didn't get up, he wheeled himself out of the room. He was in a wheelchair. *How did I miss that?*

"I'm sorry. When I was in your dream, I left what we call a seed, and orchestrated things so that you would fall asleep on the ride to the base. I hope now you'll be content with a simple blindfold. Also, here's your cell phone."

"Is that really necessary?"

"I'm afraid it is, for now. After next weekend it'll be okay for you to learn everyone's real names, and how to get here yourself. But for now, we have to follow protocol. It's how we've remained safe."

"Safe from what..." then Akira answered his own question. "The Dark Man?"

"A question with an answer for a different time. Let's get you back to school now."

"Alright. I still have lots of questions that need answers though, okay Sniper?" He giggled at her codename. She laughed back sarcastically, then handed him his backpack and a blindfold with her own sardonic smile. It was riddled in mockery.

CHAPTER 20

AKIRA RETURNED TO HIS DORM in the late hours of Friday night. Saturday morning was a more accurate and technical time frame, but Akira refused to call the night morning until after he went to bed. He could barely even process all that happened. It truly felt like it was all a bunch of dreams inside of one dream. He was living that old movie, *Inception*. He'd wake up soon, and his mom would still be alive. Amy would still be his girlfriend. He would wake up and tell one of them--or both of them, that he just had the longest and craziest dream ever.

But no, Akira knew it was impossible for a dream to be so intricate. So long. All of it was real, which meant the entirety of the past six months were without a doubt real. *It was his reality.* His interior struggle was interrupted when Corey bumped into Akira on his way out of the room. He looked upset.

"Oh, Akira! Hey man. Where have you been?"

"I uh, well I was visiting some family friends in New Jersey."

"Gross! Man, Jersey sucks," Corey said. "Anyway, I think I'm going to request a room change. I can't stand Ray anymore. Anytime we've been in the dorm at the same time he would find some way to make fun of me," Corey swallowed audibly. "He even said he wishes that I was the one who went missing instead of you."

"Damn. That's pretty harsh. I'll try talking to him."

"Yeah, whatever AK-47. See you."

Tempted as he was to ask Corey where he was heading this late (or early), Akira was simply too tired. Five days of classes until his next meet with the mysterious MLK. Did they all have powers too? What kind of training did they mean? Akira had so many questions. He thought it might end up being difficult to remain focused during class. And what of Sid Meyers? Should he confront him, or are they going to act like Friday night never happened? Akira had also decided that Sid was most likely the cocky figure who reached out to him during his first night at college.

"Man, life is weird." he muttered as he walked into his dorm room and prepared to embrace sleep without dreamwalking. Or dream shifting, or whatever the crazies out there were calling it these days.

• • •

It was a cold Wednesday. Wednesday was the day that the Robotics Engineering Club met. Akira and Lauren met up and went together.

"Did you read the email? Apparently we're going to get our bot designations today. We'll either build small bots individually or larger ones in small groups."

As Lauren spoke of large bots, Akira couldn't help but think of the giant life-size mech that Sid was inside of. How his suit repaired a hole in his chest for him seamlessly.

"I'm awful at keeping up with emails." Akira said. The classroom was in sight down the hallway now.

"Which type of bot do you think you'll want to build?" he asked her.

"I like 'em big!" She answered flirtatiously. Akira only smiled awkwardly and nodded. They entered the classroom and Akira immediately locked eyes with Sid. He gave a tough look back, then lowered his eyes to Lauren and his face became warm and fragile.

"Hayyy!" he said. Akira nearly forgot that they were an item. *Why did I come back here again..?*

"Alright lady-nerds and gentlemanly virgins, today I'm going to assign you to your teams. I know some of you have requested to work solo or in a group specifically, but since our club is recognized in the Tri-state area as the best around, I may or may not have ignored your wimpy futile requests."

Akira wondered if he'd ever be able to get over how smug Sid was. *Entitled prick.* He thought, and not for the first time.

"Okay. Groups first. Group Alpha will be, me, the beautiful girl with reddish-brown hair and a face that could kill, Herbert, and Akira."

Akira was a bit surprised because he put himself down for individual. He figured he'd work by himself and impress Lauren and emasculate Sid. Besides getting selected for a group rather than individual work, he was frankly surprised Sid decided to put him into his group. He looked at the "beautiful girl with reddish brown hair" and Lauren said "Don't look at me! I didn't ask him to put you with us, but that's still awesome right?"

Riiight. Akira smiled and produced a nod. Sid finished announcing the rest of the groups. Then he told the groups to meet, and solo builders to leave at their own discretion. Akira sat at the large wooden block they called a table until Sid finished answering his peons' questions and waltzed over.

"Hello Akira, long time no see,"

"Not long enough." Akira replied, but Sid Meyers was already pretending to cough, which he transformed into a mild choke. Akira knew he was mocking him, but Herbert, being the kiss ass he is circled behind Sid and started patting his back.

"Get off me!" Sid said while brushing him off.

"So Herbert, did your mom have to call Sid for you to get put on this team?"

Lauren joked, but an unfazed Herbert replied "Nope, my skills are just of the highest level of achievement. I'd say that's a better reason to be here than, um, well sleeping the head of the club. Haha, it's almost nepotism!" He laughed at his own observation, until he observed that Sid was giving him a death stare. He quickly swallowed a lump in his throat, which Akira would not have been too surprised if the lump happened to of been Sid's load from before class. Then he frowned at the dirty thought and wondered if college made him a tad bit cruder than before.

A solemn thought crossed his mind, that the last of the innocent Akira had died with his mom. He wasn't an adolescent anymore, and he hadn't thought about how much he grew over the summer until now.

"Alright that's enough monkeying around. I've selected you three to be a part of this group because you three are the best in the club. Now let's talk business."

The four of them decided to make a bot on treads, that can follow you around and play music or answer questions with its limited AI interface. Sid dismissed everyone, who now had ideas of what they were doing. Each person knew what their role in the group was, but Sid still told Akira to stay. Lauren smiled, likely thinking about how happy she was that they were getting along now. She left, practically dragged Herbert out with her. He was staring at Akira with envy scribbled all over his face.

"So. You met with the MLK over the weekend didn't you? After my fight, I didn't sense you in that hotel. You were on the move. I figure you even left the state, because I have pretty good range capabilities my very Asian friend."

Akira thought about it, and he guessed it was kind of a fight. That didn't dawn on him until now. Then he rolled his eyes at the harmless and purposeless mention of his ethnicity.

"Yeah, maybe I did, what of it?"

"I wanna know everything. Also, are you Chinese or Japanese? I've narrowed my guess down to those two."

Akira scoffed. "Pft. Why would I tell you anything, and what would I get out of doing so?"

These people trust me. I can't do anything to put them in harm's way.

"And for your information, I'm both."

Sid nodded, clearly pleased with himself. "I could teach you about sensing other shifters. How to unlock your potential. You don't know them. They could be using you. Just like a tool, then they'll throw you away when they're finished."

Akira visibly considered the notion. "Well, you didn't threaten to kick me out of the club like I expected, because then I'd be out of here quicker than a white guy in a Math class. But no, you do have a valid point. I'll consider it Meyers."

If all goes well, they'll teach me about sensing others anyway. So I just need to play my cards right and be careful..

"You do that Kishimoto. You know where I'll be." Sid said through a half smirk. He watched Akira turn and go.

• • •

On Friday, Akira went to Madison Square Garden and met Kristen. She walked with him a few blocks away to where the car was. In New York City, a few blocks when it comes to parking is typically at least ten of the suburban blocks he was accustomed to. There they got into her car, and she blindfolded him again before they departed. She told him that it would be nice if this was the last time that Akira had to get blindfolded. The perverted hetero-sexual teenager lurking beneath his conscious thoughts silently disagreed.

Akira was released from his visual captivity in the same place as last time. He got out of the car in the garage, but this time Kristen was waiting with him. "I hope you're ready for this kid, because it's not going to be easy."

He nodded and followed her throughout the base. He was able to take in the sleek details of the base a little better now that he wasn't trying to sneak around undetected anymore.

"So are you going to be the one training me?" He asked, with a sliver of hopefulness in his voice.

"Nope. I might be teaching you or lecturing you similar to your professors but I'm not qualified nor suited to train you."

"Why is that?" Akira asked, as they entered the kitchen.

"My abilities as a Dream Shifter are well, limited,"

Akira thought back to the battle he witnessed outside his apart-ment. It certainly didn't seem like she had limited abilities back then. Even the all-powerful and cocky Sid Meyers and his freaking robot showed fear at her threats.

"My sensory range is very long distance. That is where my strength lies, and that is why I am codenamed Sniper. In shifter to shifter combat, I am less than extraordinary. Blizzard on the other hand, is extremely skilled."

They entered the circular room and Blizzard was sitting down looking at his phone again. The phone he's allowed to keep on him, meanwhile Kristen is still holding onto his. Akira thought about how he purposely bumped into him on his way out not even a week ago. *Blizzard and Sid would probably make a good couple,* Akira thought to cheer himself up.

"Kristen my dear," he said still watching his phone.

"Yes?"

"Leave us."

She nodded as if he were looking at her, even though he wasn't. She turned to leave the room and then said "If you have any questions or need anything, let me know."

"Sure thing," Akira answered. He knew Kristen couldn't hold his hand throughout the entirety of his training. He was prepared to prove himself to her, to Jack and anyone else that doubted him.

"Okay Bruce Lee. Let's get started."

He led Akira out of the room into another room. It was profusely dark, but Akira was able to make out what looked like about four beds. Or coffins. He was definitely hoping they were the former.

"Get started with what? I thought you were going to train me, not seduce me?"

Blizzard shoved him into the dark room.

"Lie down. I'm going to administer a perfectly safe amount of sleeping gas into an oxygen mask that will drop onto your lap in two seconds."

Akira sat on a bed and the oxygen mask hit his head and fell to his lap.

"But-"

"Sh. I'm not finished. You are untrained. We can't wait forever for you to fall asleep or to reach a tranquil meditative state. I'm going to shift into your mind. That is where the real training will happen, got it?"

"Yeah." Akira put on the gas mask and heard Blizzard flip a switch somewhere. Within a minute, he was inhaling the infamous sleeping gas and being put down under.

"Let's see what you're made of Bruce."

Akira's eyes were almost adjusted to the darkness by the time he started blinking. It was only a slight change of darkness. He heard Blizzard say something about pee made of spruce. Then he was in the land of dreams.

CHAPTER 21

To go from nearly pitch black to vivid color was something Akira was getting used to as a dreamwalker, or shall we say as a Dream Shifter. However, he was not prepared to go from the blackness of a tire-up-close to a large blank sheet of paper. After vision kicked in, physical sensations came next. Akira immediately felt numbingly cold. The chill hit his face first, then his poor selection of footwear came next. Within seconds his feet felt wet and disconnected. Tilting his head up, Akira took in his surroundings. All around him were mountains of various sizes. More than just the peaks were capped with snow and ice. In fact, everywhere Akira looked was covered in snow other than a few trees that were showing off specific patterns of leafless wood.

Because of the 360 degree turn Akira did to take in his desolate and frozen surroundings, he was all the more surprised when he got kicked in the back and was propelled face first into snow. *As if my face wasn't cold enough already, but hey it beats sand.*

He immediately took his face out and turned while simultaneously brushing some remnants of snow off of his face. Blizzard was standing on a single metallic stone that was jutting out of the snow at an angle.

"First things first. Have you ever taken any fighting classes? Karate, wrestling, boxing, MMA, Taekwondo, anything of the sort?"

Akira noticed that Blizzard was in a winter coat and boots with thick cold-resistant gloves, probably army issue. He wasn't wearing any of that before. Akira looked down and as expected, was wearing the clothes he fell asleep in. Warm, but not exactly the kind of stuff you'd wear when you make a snowman.

"I did karate when I was younger. I only made it to Orange Belt. That was years ago. I've also been going to the gym more frequently than ever."

"Great," Blizzard said. Akira smiled. "More work for me then."

His smile faded. Then he got kicked from behind him again. And he was sent spiraling forward again. When he turned to look, no one was there. Blizzard was still next to the stone, although now he was audibly walking towards Akira. "Lesson one. Don't call me Blizzard. You haven't earned it yet. My name is Todd Rimando. I'm nineteen years old. I may only be a year older than you, but trust me I'm superior to you in every way. Lesson Two will start once you can knock me down." Akira didn't like the smile he produced. He interpreted it to mean that Todd didn't think Akira could do that.

Akira charged through about six inches of snow, ignoring his semi-numb feet. The deep snow slowed his speed, so when he was within about a foot of Todd he jumped at him, hoping to bring him down the ground with him. As he left the ground time slowed. He saw Todd look at the snow in front of him, then pull both his feet out of the snow they were in. His boots stepped on the spot he just looked at like it was as solid as a rock. Then he jumped forward towards Akira. Akira believed he had just enough time to change from a tackle to a punch. As he put his fist into a ball, Todd's hands were already on his shoulders and he pushed Akira downwards as he did a front flip over him and landed at the location where Akira jumped from.

Floating in mid-air, Akira braced himself for the pain of falling face first into the ice Todd jumped from, but Akira fell through it like it was snow. As he got close, he noted that Todd didn't even leave a boot print. He collided with the snow and although he avoided pain, his face plummeted through the bitter cold pile of frozen water.

He got up as quickly as he could. Todd was smiling. Akira knew he was skinny, but what he just did was impossible!

"How did you do that Blizzard?"

"I told you, my name is Todd. Earn the right to call me Blizzard, or kiss my tracks in the snow you damn fool."

Todd lifted his gloved hand towards Akira and a pile of snow transmuted into a fist and was propelled into his gut. He was lifted off the ground and sent flying back into the snow for a third time. The hand felt more like ice than snow. Akira had the wind knocked out of him. Then the fist became powdery snow and collapsed on his stomach leaving him looking like he got knocked over by a loosely crafted snowball.

"You've left me less than impressed. I don't know what Kristen and Jack see in you. All I see is a wimp who can't even lay a finger on me."

He closed his eyes and tilted his head down. Sighing, he said "Don't question what is and what isn't possible here. I can see it in your face. This is all a dream. Your dream technically too. You have the home field advantage. Use it."

Akira stood up. The scattered snow on his face looked like white freckles. Some of the water made it look like he was crying. He focused on repeating Todd's snow fist trick. He pictured it in his head but it wasn't working. Then he thought back to some of his experiments. He pictured he had a baseball bat. He imagined it. Wished for it. Blue squares in the outline of a baseball bat began appearing and vibrating and connected with one another. Once they were complete and all touching each other, the color faded and gave way to the crisp brown of the wooden baseball bat Akira now held in his hands.

Akira somehow felt like he was cheating, but Todd was being a dick and he had this coming from the start. Akira charged at him once more, narrowly dodging a frozen block of ice shaped like a boot that was launched at him. As he was closing the distance Todd held out a finger and a blueish beam shot out. It looked like blue lightning. It hit the snow in front of him and disappeared. When Akira's foot landed in that spot mid run, he didn't step through the snow; instead his foot slid backward and he fell forward help-lessly. He used his right side and his arm to break his fall.

The pain was immense. His hip bone and his arm felt stiff with pain throughout.

Akira was done with this icy tundra and the hellishly cold cli-mate that came with it. *Time to try something I learned back in Jake's dream.* Akira closed his eyes and put his hands outward. The bat was on the ice he slipped on. Blue beams shot out of his hands go-ing all the way to the mountains that surrounded them. The beams expanded out onto the snow on the ground and up the mountains of both sides. Akira gave them both a yank and it looked like Akira tore a dimension out on both sides. Behind the picture-like im-age of mountains that was now torn, it looked like a sea of end-less black. Then Akira created a sunny field which now took the place of the black background behind the torn mountains. Akira's string of energy was stuck to the background that looked like a picture, and he was trying to tear it down.

Todd stood there doing his best to keep his astonishment to himself. He remembered how hard it was to learn how to change the scenery of a dream. He also was sure he wouldn't forget how hard it was to do that in a dream where you weren't the sole shifter. Todd closed his eyes and sent out pulses of invisible energy to maintain the mountain scenery he created. Without moving, he put the rips of the two sides back into place slowly. Akira's blue energy receded back into his hands as the rest of the tear was covered up. This eclipsed his sunny field background until it was erased from existence. Although Todd appeared to do this effortlessly since he did it standing still, he still utilized a lot of his energy to do it. He opened his eyes and watched Akira drop to his knees.

"My power over ice while dream shifting comes from my upbringing, and I guess maybe my personality too."

Akira put one hand on his knee and forced himself up.

"I was born and raised in a small town you never heard of outside of Anchorage, Alaska. Most of my childhood memories have snow in them. Some Dream Shifters have unique powers that can't be replicated. The ice power is mine. We're going to find out if you have one too, although it's never easy to figure out."

Akira walked over to Todd. "How did you first find out your unique power?"

"I was shifting in someone's dream when I lost control. It flipped over and became a nightmare. I had to protect the person who's dream I invaded, and it was all my fault. Instinct kicked in, and now I'm the second strongest Dream Shifter in the MLK."

Akira thought about it, and wondered if Jack or Kristen was stronger than Todd. Then Todd vanished. Akira quickly panicked, then Todd jumped out of the snow in front of him and slammed Akira's chin with an uppercut. Akira's body actually lifted out of the snow from the impact. Todd used the momentum to spin his body and then send out a roundhouse kick into Akira's chest changing his body's trajectory. He landed with a loud thwump displacing snow all around him. When he stood up, the snow looked like a chalk outline from a murder movie. Then Todd was behind Akira and Akira could vaguely sense that his hands were hovering over his head.

"Let's see what's in the old noggin, huh Bruce Lee?"

How can I beat someone that's so fast? How can he move through the snow like that?

Before Akira could react, ice came up his legs and encased his entire body except his head. It was bitter cold. Akira couldn't even move a finger. He never felt so trapped in his entire life, and he had a feeling Todd was about to rape his way into his memories.

Blue energy emanated from Todd's fingers and he closed his eyes to process the information he sorted through.

With his eyes still closed, Todd spoke.

"Wow, I took you for a nerd. How did you ever get this Amy girl? She's gorgeous. Like model-gorgeous."

Akira squirmed. "Get out of my head! NO ONE INVITED YOU IN THERE."

"She's trying to do makeup her whole life? Pfttt. She should be an actress. She looks like one of those hot girls' sitcom leads are always dating."

"Shut up. I didn't consent to this!" *Am I just stuck here to endure him torturing me? Can he see what I'm thinking right now, because if he can then know this: I fucking hate you Todd. I hate you so much right now.*

Todd let out a loud whistle. "God damn, she's even better looking naked. It's like I'm watching amateur softcore porn in here ahahaha." The laughing made him think of Dmitri with his invisible fingers wrapped around his throat. To access his memories is one thing, but to access those personal memories that he kept tucked deep in his subconscious was a completely different thing.

Akira was losing it. How could the MLK let this sicko in their ranks? He swung his head back hoping to head-butt him but he barely even touched the fingers that were still hovering centimeters above his head.

"Wow. Your mom died recently. That sucks. You're guilty that you didn't see her more in the hospital. You're worried you were a letdown to her." Todd seemed to consider this for a second, or perhaps he was just focused on what was inside Akira's head.

"I think you're right to think that. You probably were a shitty son. Half your mourning period was spent thinking about how you lost that Amy chick."

Todd expected to get a rise out of Akira from that but he didn't. Then his connection to Akira's memories was severed against his will. He opened his eyes and did a front flip over the frozen statue of Akira. Todd couldn't believe what he was seeing. Akira's eyes were glowing blue. Todd couldn't even see his pupils anymore.

"YOU FUCKING ASSHOLE," Akira screamed and the ice shattered into millions of fragments. Todd back flipped away and used his arm to protect his eyes. Then he felt heat. And a lot of it. He saw at the edges of his arm a bright orange tint.

Removing his arm from it's protective position he was frightened for the first time in a long time. His eyes reflected the image he now took in. Akira was surrounded by a ring of fire. Flames danced around him. They swirled with an atavistic hunger up to four feet into the sky.

Now things have gotten interesting.

CHAPTER 22

THE SNOW AROUND AKIRA MELTED away. It looked like he was surrounded by a large water colored donut.

"Interesting...few have escaped my ice prison."

Akira stepped toward Todd. As he got closer to the ring of fire it parted itself for him. Now it was a crescent moon of fire. "Take back what you said." he ordered. The voice didn't sound like Akira anymore. Todd took an unconscious step back.

Is his unique power over fire? This could prove extra dangerous to me. Still, it's my job to help him reach his potential. Besides, Todd Rimando never backs down from a fight. Let's see if he's worth training after all.

After a moment of silence other than the sounds of flames dancing, Todd replied.

"No."

The semi-circle of fire surrounding Akira flared upwards, melting more snow in the process.

Akira stepped out of the ring and held up his left hand. Todd thought he saw a tattoo on the palm of Akira's hand that he neglected to notice before. Although he was unable to see what the tattoo was, Todd did notice it begin to glow blue. Then the fire behind Akira shot forward at him. Todd shoved his hands down into the snow in front of him and a ten foot wall of ice came up in front of him.

He never truly felt cold. In fact, this weather was warm to him. He estimated it to be about thirty degrees Fahrenheit. The fire slammed into the ice wall and melted away about two inches of the wall's thickness. One inch remained. When the fire subsided, Todd shot his arm out like a punch towards the wall. Instead of his knuckle hitting it, the wall of ice began sliding forward as if it were on wheels. The further away from Todd, the faster it went. Akira dove to the side and narrowly dodged it. After the wall passed where it would have connected with Akira's face, it ran over Akira's fiery crescent and dowsed the flames. Then it simply tilted over and landed in the snow with a *thud*. The wall melted away immediately after.

When Akira still made no move to get up, Todd decided to boil some more of the boy's blood. "Your mother's a whore."

Todd expected him to get up and lunge at him. Instead he was still face down in the snow.

"Well Bruce Lee. You've impressed me, I'll give you that. Unfortunately, I still don't think you have what it takes to-"

"STOP CALLING ME THAT!" Akira said through his teeth, despite still being face down in snow. Todd was fascinated as he watched the level of snow around Akira drop as it melted. Todd was more than fascinated when a fireball the size of a baseball came out of the snow in front of him and detonated right before it hit him in the stomach.

As Todd was thrown back about five feet from the force of the small explosion he mused about the surprise. *Somehow he focused his energy enough to send a tiny ball of fire melting through snow like a drill without me noticing. It traversed the distance between him and I unnoticed before it popped out at me. The advanced level of concentration and psychic control that must have taken is pretty astounding.*

Todd was now lying on his back in the snow. He thought back to when he was a kid. Making snow angels back then was so fun, but it snowed so often in Alaska that it lost its spark when he was about five. Sometimes when he was a teenager he'd drink himself stupid and then lie in the snow and think about life until he actually did feel cold.

Even though he is only nineteen, after learning about his power and then eventually the MLK, Todd has since considered himself an adult. He hasn't been on his back in the snow thinking about life in the entirety of the two years he's had his powers. Then he snapped back to reality and remembered Akira. He got up and Akira was still face down.

"Hey." No answer.

"Yo Akira." Still nothing.

I guess it's time to snap back to reality.

Todd severed the connection and used a subtle psychic nudge that should have woken Akira up as well.

• • •

Todd immediately opened his eyes after that. He turned on the lights and walked over to Akira. Still in his bed, Akira didn't react to the lights. Todd put his hand on his neck and felt a pulse. He started shaking him from the shoulders. A thought occurred to him suddenly, and he lifted up Akira's left hand. There was no tattoo on his palm.

"Wake up."

Still nothing.

Todd was annoyed at the idea of having to go get Kristen or Jack for help. He stood in the doorway with his back to what was designated as the Meditation Chamber, when Akira said "Good morning."

"Do you remember anything?" Todd asked while turning around. Akira yawned.

"No, nothing." His pupils shifted to the top left corner of each of his eyes. "Wait, I remember being cold. There was some snow, and I think you wanted me to knock you down. Did I succeed?"

Todd considered it for a second. *He really doesn't remember when he went berserk, does he?*

"HA just kidding! I know I whooped your ass. You had a butt full of snow. I didn't see it, but I could feel it. I just figured it'd be funny to do the 'hero kicks butt so hard without self-control then can't remember any of it' trope." Akira smiled.

Todd's eyes were in shock. It was the most surprised Todd has looked since Akira met him and he decided to savor every moment of it.

Todd turned to walk out of the room.

"Hey wait!" Akira called but Todd already left. He assumed he was going to report to Jack or Kristen how he did. Akira hoped it would be a positive report. Thinking back, he honestly was pretty scared. He couldn't remember the last time he had so little control over his body like that. During some of the action, Akira actually watched himself from outside of his body. It was awesome, scary, and well---unbelievable. Akira remembered thinking it was like playing as himself in a third-person video game. He got off the bed and walked out the door. Before he could go searching for Todd, Kristen appeared.

"So, I hear you had an interesting time."

"I sure did. I guess I have a unique power after all."

She put her hand on his shoulder and gently nodded her head.

"Come with me. I think Jack is going to let you become a member. I'm going to save you time and get some of your questions answered."

She led him to the conference room with the large table that looked like it belonged in an executive corporate suite.

He took a seat before she even suggested it.

"So," she began. Akira was able to detect that she had a speech organized in her head but by the time it actually came down to the order of things, it got mixed up.

"It's always hard knowing where to start with these things," she admitted.

"The MLK was founded back in 1998 by Marco Peterson. He wasn't the most creative guy around, but he had a good heart and a good head on his shoulders. When he realized he had powers, the first thing he wanted to do was use them to help people."

Akira reflected on his "experiments" and the time he daydreamed about using his powers to make women interested in him. He thought about when he slept with Amy in her dream. *I never said I was the most moral person around.* Still, he felt a pang of guilt.

"Since that day in 1998, we have run a business where we help people with insomnia and sleep paralysis. Basically, if you're have sleeping problems, we can help you without medication. They do not know that we heal them with our powers. We do this upstairs in a doctor's office. That way we can help people, and create revenue. We are not a part of the government. We had to spend our own money to build this large secretive basement. Luckily one of us is an official doctor as well. The only other goal is to find rogue Dream Shifters such as yourself and persuade them to join us. If they are the selfish type like your friend Sid, then we assign one of our own to follow them."

"How many members of the MLK are there?" Akira asked. Between the size of what is apparently only a basement and the magnitude of what Kristen was saying, Akira guessed there would be about fifty members.

Kristen closed her eyes and thought about it.

"We had eighteen active members. In the last year four have gone MIA and two are confirmed...dead." Kristen seemed to choke on the last word. Akira was sure it had a bad taste in her mouth.

"Holy crap, that's it?"

"We've always been a small operation. But that Dark Man has been hunting us down. He caused two fatal vehicular accidents. One member was forced to fall asleep while riding his motorcycle on the freeway. He died in the ICU. The other..well we believe he had some very important documents on him. He tried sending messages to us but they kept getting intercepted. He was my boyfriend, and Jack's second in command." A tear threatened to jump down her cheek, but it held its position, making her eyes gleam.

"I'm so sorry Kristen."

"Sometimes this world just isn't fair. But I will honor his memory and cherish the times we had," as she held back more tears from streaming she asked "Do you have any other questions?"

"Yeah. Why do you call yourselves Dream Shifters? And in a battle between two Dream Shifters, what happens when one wins?"

"Well a shifter could be defined as a stagehand in a play who is responsible for moving scenery. When Marco first discovered his power it was one of the first things he learned he could do. We didn't know about the fights until about a decade after the MLK was founded. To answer your other question, we believe the science of it is that the intellectual prowess and the spirit or soul fuse into one force and that gives the shifter their unique powers. When two Dream Shifters are in the same dream their powers are battling behind the scenes before they even fight. The fight only pushes the balance to an earlier climax. In a sense, it weakens the loser's powers so that the victor has total control. Another power of a Dream Shifter is to prevent someone from retreating. Therefore, a variety of things could happen. One of the most common is the victor might trap someone in their own dream. This would lead to a coma-like state in the real world. Another advanced technique would be to disrupt cognitive function, so when the loser of the fight wakes up they might be brain dead or mentally unstable. Because of the nature of these things, we obviously have not tested them out intricately, this is mostly from data we've collected."

Kristen took a coffee out of a mini fridge and walked it over to the microwave.

"What do you mean intricately? So the MLK has used these methods before?"

"We refrain from murder. But we have had to deal with dangerous rogues over the years. Sean even solved a murder case once. There were some that used the aforementioned technique to make them unfit to do anything in the real world. They would then be transported to a psychiatric facility where they would be harmless and catered to. Trust me when I say that these people were dangers to society and this was the only solution. Even if we managed to imprison a rogue Dream Shifter they are still a danger."

Akira chewed on his cheek inside his mouth. This is tougher than when controversial topics were brought up in school. *I'm pro-choice. War is evil, but sometimes necessary. Religion was originally created to manipulate, but now it has enriched millions of lives.* But this? Kristen was talking about making people mentally ill or putting them in comas. But she did have a point, even if Akira was in jail he could still touch people's dreams. He imagined a scenario where he gets to know a prison guard well enough and then gives him a subtle dream push to unlock Akira's cell. Obviously it wouldn't be that easy but it's still a danger the MLK has to consider.

"Come on. I think it's time you met our on-base members. I'll continue with our little lecture while we walk."

As they turned to leave the room Akira noticed that Todd was listening in and leaning against the wall.

"Here's Todd Rimando. I know you two hit it off already. Todd is nineteen years old and was born in Alaska. When we discovered him we had him move closer, so he lives here on the base. Todd has seventeen wins and three losses under his belt. That includes fights in the field, and full-length sparring matches."

"Does that include our little scrimmage?"

Todd rolled his eyes. "You make me want to die." Then he left the room.

"As you've seen, Todd's unique power is that of ice. We have to accept that the obvious answer is because he's been around it his whole life in Alaska. Okay, moving on." *She's quite the tour guide,* Akira thought and chuckled.

Akira was starting to zone out. He wanted to test out his unique powers again. *Why can I control fire? I wasn't born in Arizona, nor was I born in Hell, I was born on Long Island.*

They passed a bathroom as they were walking. In it, a mirror and sink were propped down lower than usual. The man in the wheelchair was brushing his teeth and paying no mind to the duo who stopped outside the bathroom.

"This is Reiner Ulrich. He is the first member of MLK to be recruited outside of the U.S. When I met him, I had to keep a German-English dictionary with me. His English has improved since then. He is twenty-three years old. Codename is Boxer. Ten wins and no losses. He is currently undefeated."

"Um. How?" Akira asked, looking at her face and then Reiner's wheelchair.

He wheeled over to them. "Guten tag my friends!" Akira shook his hand.

"Reiner was training to be a professional boxer in his home country. He's from Frankfurt, I think. Then a bad car accident crippled him. His nerves and anxiety brought back his childhood asthma. However, when he dream shifts, he has use of his legs and his asthma is non-existent."

"Ooooh. That must be awesome man." And Akira thought *he* couldn't wait to use his powers, dreams were the only place where Reiner had control of his legs.

"Nein. It is *very* awesome." He said with a proud smile. Then he wheeled himself past them. "Reiner was actually one of the three people to beat Todd. Reiner's physical prowess is pretty unbelievable."

Akira figured he'd have to be pretty unbelievable to beat Todd in a fight. He himself had barely been able to knock him down, let alone defeat him in a full fight. Kristen led him to a door under an EXIT sign, but behind the door was a staircase. She typed in a four-digit code and the door opened. Akira didn't know of any other EXIT doors that required codes. They walked up a medium sized staircase. The door at the end was locked from where they stood, clearly to prevent anyone from accidentally wandering down there.

"This is the doctor's office. It's closed on weekends."

Akira marveled at how realistic everything looked. The waiting room looked so..*average*. There were magazines on tables, a sign that read **CO-PAY MUST BE PAID THE DAY OF AN APPOINTMENT-NO EXCEPTIONS.** The sliding glass window that separated the office from the waiting room was closed and locked. They entered the door next to the reception window. It read: **PLEASE WAIT UNTIL YOU HAVE BEEN CALLED.**

Akira counted two patient examination rooms, one break room complete with a fridge, a table and a sink. Akira mused at how small the table was compared to the one downstairs. There were two bathrooms next to each other, but instead of being separated by genders they were separated for customers and employees. At the end of the semicircle hallway that went around the reception area, was a medium sized office. Sitting there working on his computer was an elderly brown man. Akira guessed he was Indian or Pakistani. On the desk was a nametag that read: **Dr. Abhi J. Ahmad MD.**

"Ah! Hello there Kristen! Is this the young man Jack had spoken of?"

Dr. Ahmad stroked his whitish-black beard.

"Yes Doctor. His name is Akira Kishimoto."

"Pleasure to meet you doctor."

They shook hands.

"Unlike our friend Reiner, Dr. Ahmad was already an American citizen by the time we recruited him. He hails from northern India. He is forty-seven years young, and the only member of MLK to have any children."

Akira observed a picture on his desk of him and two children. Beside him is a happy looking wife.

"If you're going to speak of my old age, you should at least mention my track record too Ms. Pierce."

She laughed. "My apologies Doctor. He has won twenty-six battles and lost nineteen. Believe it or not, but his codename is also Doctor."

Akira could believe that, but he was still struggling to try to imagine this man who's almost fifty fighting youngsters.

"As you've heard I've had my experience of battling. Judging by my win to loss ratio you've probably also figured out that I'm a much better healer."

"Dr. Ahmad runs the entire front practically single handed. If I'm on base, I'll help as a nurse or pretend doctor. I'm only an LPN but I can help some of our smaller cases. Our other associate who you haven't met yet codenamed Tigress often helps out in reception, or Todd if he owes us a favor."

Akira let out a laugh at that. "I love the idea of that guy having to pick up phones and put people on hold."

"You should see it sometime." Kristen said with a smile.

"So tell me more about yourself." Akira asked as they made their way back to the lower levels, leaving the Doctor to his computer and the paperwork on the screen.

"You mean more about me?" She gave a light sigh. "Well, I guess I could reintroduce myself in the same manner as the others. My name is Kristen Pierce, and I am thirty-one years old. My codename is-"

"Holy shit!" Akira blurted. She looked startled. "Wh-what? What's wrong?"

Embarrassed, Akira said "Oh. Um. Well I just thought you were like in your mid-twenties 'sall. Like twenty-four tops."

Her worried face quickly became a smile. "Well you're certainly sweet. Maybe a good actor, but sweet nonetheless."

Before he could prove it was genuine, she was back on track. Akira didn't want to keep interrupting her.

"I'm codenamed Sniper because my range is the longest of all the shifters at the MLK. Not only can I sense someone that is dream shifting over two hundred miles away, but I can also shift into their dreams as well. I was in New Jersey when I interrupted your dreams. Unfortunately, despite this and some healing abilities, I cannot fight like other Dream Shifters. I am simply too weak. Because of this, I have no records of my battle history."

"I see." said Akira, who did not actually see. He thought her powers were impressive. Was making The Dark Man retreat not a victory? Kristen was reaching for the door at the end of the staircase when someone else opened it.

She was beautiful. No, pretty. No, scratch that, gorgeous. Akira couldn't make up his mind about the striking blonde haired girl that entered the stairwell. Her green eyes stared straight past them. When Kristen motioned towards her, the eyes softly scanned Akira. His eyes went to the door beside her. "Ah, this is Kara. She must have just arrived. Going up to talk to Doctor?"

She nodded her head.

"Nice to meet you," Akira said with his hand out.

The beautiful girl named Kara nodded her head again and took his hand. The soft touch of her hand was comforting. He smiled when he let her hand go, but her face remained devoid of emotion. She walked past him and began climbing up the stairs. They went back to the room where Kristen began lecturing. "Don't worry Akira. She's always quiet and timid, especially around new people. Her codename is Tigress. She has one win and one loss."

Akira sat down at the large table. He expected Kristen to lecture more, really she could have been a great teacher. Instead, Jack came in. "Stand up." Akira stood.

"Welcome to the MLK, Kishimoto."

CHAPTER 23

"YOU ARE NOW A LOW level member of the MLK. You're a novice level shifter. An apprentice, if you will. So you will have less than full access to our databases and operations. You will abide by the order of command. You will do what is right, and your primary duty will be to ensure Mr. Peterson's dreams for the future come true. From henceforth, you take on a variety of new responsibilities including trustworthy use of your powers; upholding an oath of secrecy, and a strict loyalty to your comrades. MLK may be a secret, but what you do still reflects us as a whole. Despite this, we will still hold you accountable for any wrongdoings within the group itself. Please do not taint our image." Jack said, then gave off a salute.

Akira stood with his back stretched. He felt taller than ever before.

"Understood. I accept all of those terms." He gave off a return salute feeling kind of weird. At times like this he still wasn't that sure if he was going to wake up or not. He quietly wished he was at least an ex-boy scout or something so the saluting didn't feel so.. *phony.*

"Take this, and never lose it. Never lend it to anyone, don't even let anyone see it. It's a key into our network that you can access anywhere. It leaves no traces. But it can be broken into if stolen. Since the death of our unspoken second in command Sean Singer, we have been using these to keep in contact with each other and to keep everyone updated."

Akira opened his hand and Jack put a USB drive in it then wrapped both of his hands around Akira's open hand. "Don't fuck up Firefly."

Akira's face dropped. "Oh man, can I get another nickname? I don't like that one!"

"We'll see." Jack turned and left. Kristen walked over and shook his hand. "Congrats Akira. Your training is still in progress though."

Akira jumped a little when Todd spoke. He snuck in the room. "I'll take it from here. Let's go to the fitness room."

"Good luck. I'll see you two around." Kristen left heading towards the kitchen and garage.

Todd led him into a room filled with workout equipment, weights, treadmills and a wall encompassing mirror. There was also a medium-sized fighting ring that Todd climbed into. He took off his shirt and threw it. Todd made sure to prove his physical dominance as well as his superior agility as he bested Akira in several different martial arts forms.

"I'm going to teach you the basics to many styles. You can't learn them all in one day, but I'm going to drill you on them until your reflexes respond positively." After three hours of Todd beating the snot out of Akira, he showed him to a room where he could spend the night. Akira enjoyed the relaxing downtime even though he was very bored. His body was sorer than ever. It was like all of his solo workouts rolled into one. Utter exhaustion was like extra weight on his body, pinning him to the bed. Right as he almost fell asleep, Kristen came in and gave him his phone back. At precisely 10:59 PM Akira finally dosed off.

• • •

Akira woke up in an alleyway. But now that his unique powers had emerged, he wasn't even a little disoriented. He knew that the MLK didn't harvest his organs and drop him in an alleyway. No, he immediately knew this was a dream. It didn't just feel like a dream; he could sense the dreamlike qualities. Almost like the air tasted different here. Now Akira could sense the difference between reality and a dream. Pleased with himself, he took in his environment. Mean and cold concrete ran up a wall as far as his eyes could see. On the other side was a blood-red brick wall that continued on in the same manner. Akira wondered where humpty dumpty was. The alleyway could just about fit a small car, but not much else. A figure appeared at the end. It was running towards him. "Looks like I can't even relax in my dreams, huh?" he said.

"Ja. Das rite," said a familiar voice. Akira's calm demeanor shrank and he remembered getting choked to near-death. Then he made out the figure. He noticed a six pack of abs that made any heavy drinker envious, gym shorts, running sneakers and..boxing gloves? Then he realized the face. Reiner Ulrich. He wondered if that meant Reiner was the Dark Man, but he pushed that thought out of his mind. *Reiner is not dashing at me full speed to have a conversation. Time to get your guard up.* He assumed a battle ready position. *My training continues.*

Displacing his weight into his legs, he leaned forward. Time slowed, and he watched Reiner pull back his right arm. He was ready for the rocket of a fist. He intercepted it with his raised left arm knocking the fist upwards. Akira also sidestepped to try to use Reiner's balance against him. It didn't work. He shot out a kick with his right foot into Reiner's chest. Not only did Reiner take the kick without stopping his momentum, but he rolled around it and grabbed Akira's leg with the left arm. The fist that

Akira just deflected immediately shot back down and grabbed Akira's arm. With jaw-tight grip on Akira's left leg and right arm, Reiner used his momentum and immense strength to turn left and lift Akira off the ground, then smash him back-first into the brick wall.

Akira felt pain throughout his back and spine, but he wondered if the spots where Reiner gripped him were hurting more. While he contemplated this phenomenon, Reiner jumped a foot back into the middle of the alleyway, then he jerked forward in a flash and hit Akira in the stomach with two jabs to the stomach and solar plexus, then he connected his right hook with Akira's face. Akira's head hit the wall and he slid down the rough brick in crumpled defeat. If it was a fight in real life it would have been over already. This would have clocked the fight in at forty-one seconds from when Akira blocked the initial punch Reiner threw.

However, this was a fight in a different reality, practically an entirely new dimension. In here, Akira's mind and spirit trumped his physical prowess. Akira thought about how excited Reiner must have been to use his legs in here meanwhile Reiner took out a cigarette and smoked it.

"You know, in real life I can't smoke anymore. After accident, my childhood asthma came back. Not only was I stuck in wheelchair, but my lungs shit out on me too."

Akira's head now won the prize for the most painful injury of the day. Despite himself, he used the brick wall that he just hit his head on as support to stand back up.

"I'm sorry to hear that."

"Enough pity. I walk and breathe fine here. Todd says you're tougher than you look. Prove it."

Akira held out his hand as if he were asking for a high five and closed his eyes.

Nothing.

How the hell do they do this in the movies and the comics?

With his eyes closed, Akira thought about his mom. Empty. Dark. Gone. Her face at the funeral. Her face when she was alive. He loved her and it made him want to weep, but he knew he needed to use his negative emotions to control his powers. He would be in control of his negative emotions. He had to be. Amy Hernandez. Why did she always say she was thinking of him, but she would stay with Jack? What about him wasn't good enough? Would things be different if he said he was in love with her sooner?

Reiner watched the Asian kid standing two feet in front of him with a great curiosity. He wondered if he was meditating. Then he saw a tattoo start to form on the kid's palm. It was a Japanese symbol. Or was it Chinese? After it was finished, it started to glow blue. No, his entire body was glowing blue. The tattoo became red. Then his hand caught on fire. 火

With one eyebrow raised, Reiner Ulrich slowly got back into a fighting stance. The cigarette still hung in his mouth.

Akira opened his eyes. His left hand was on FIRE. But he didn't freak out. In fact, he smiled. He felt the warmth, the heat, and most importantly-the power. But it did not burn him, because it knew he was its master. "Say cheese!" he said, as he launched a ball of fire at Reiner. He ducked with amazing reflexes. Akira didn't think his body would have been able to respond so quickly when the distance between them was so short. The fire hit the cement wall behind Reiner and splashed. Some of it dropped in little sparks or drops of fire. The rest scorched the cement wall black. Akira observed his hand was no longer on fire at the same time that Reiner noticed. Except Reiner was already in his face. He threw a jab and

Akira blocked it, but then Reiner's right hand hooked into his face again. This time though, Akira absorbed the blow and thought of how sick he was of getting beaten around. Life kicked his ass, then Todd and now Reiner? His left hand sparked again as it engulfed itself in flames.

Reiner's fist was just about rolling off of Akira's cheek when Akira launched his hand in an abducting backhand that connected with Reiner's face. Akira took great pleasure in seeing that his hand took off like an airplane leaving slight traces of flares in the air before they dissipated. The backhand charged with fire sent Reiner into a corkscrew spin backwards.

Akira also smiled when Reiner's skull slammed into the cement. *No offense buddy, but now you know concrete and brick HURT.* This time the flame remained ablaze on Akira's hand. *Wow. I pimp slapped a boxer with fire! Powers are so cool!*

Then Reiner used his feet to launch himself into the air and land back onto his feet just in time to give Akira a tackle back into the brick he was quickly becoming accustomed to. Akira decided powers were definitely awesome, but no match for Reiner's physical prowess in a confined space. That's why he had created an alleyway.

Akira pushed Reiner, then turned and ran. In his peripheral vision, he saw the disappointment on Reiner's face. Akira decided to try to press his luck on controlling his flames. He ran as fast as he could, then he flung his left hand backward. It worked. He skidded to a stop and turned around. Part of the alleyway was on fire. Reiner also slowed, wary of Akira's new powers. Akira held out his hand. It remained ablaze, and he somehow knew he could control the flame he left behind him. *Stopping was a big mistake pal* Akira thought as he caused the flame trap to expand and swallow the alleyway between the two whole. It started off the size of a campfire, but after Akira focused his pyrokinesis powers, the fire shot up both of the walls of the alleyway. The flames now danced seven feet high.

"Woah." Akira couldn't help himself. He was amazed. He barely knew what he was doing, which thrilled him even more.

Akira contemplated trying to change the environment again.

A change of scenery certainly could help. But then again, did Reiner not set himself up for a funnel of fire? Akira would be foolish to miss the opportunity to turn the alleyway into a toaster. He couldn't see Reiner behind the flames and smoke anymore. He closed his left hand into a fist and felt the flame grow stronger. Closing his hand seemed to be charging it. He opened his palm and fired. This fireball was the size of a smart car. *And way cooler err..hotter.* Akira thought. The fireball went into the makeshift barrier he made and disappeared. He sensed it go out the other end. He waited to hear a scream or yelp, but none came.

Akira moved both his hands outward as if he was doing a breast-stroke in a pool and the flames were displaced against the walls giving clear sight of the rest of the alleyway. The fireball was still going straight forward, perhaps forever since Akira didn't know if the alleyway ended in this dream. But where was Reiner? Was he incinerated?

Akira noticed an anomaly in the brick wall. He tried to clear the fire with his mind but failed. He didn't know how to make it dissipate. He began walking over to it. He got within a foot of the fire wall when he saw a hole in the wall. A human sized hole. That was when Reiner punched through the brick on the other side of the fire wall. The burst pelted Akira with bricks. One brick slammed into his jaw. Another right into the gut. One half-broken one flew into his shoulder. Akira was certain he hated bricks now.

But there was no time to worry about that because Reiner was back on him. Before Akira could do anything, Reiner delivered a swift side kick into Akira's temple and knocked him unconscious before his body even hit the ground.

CHAPTER 24

REINER USED HIS POWERS TO allow Akira a good night's rest, even in defeat. Akira woke up the next day from dreamless sleep.

"For often, when one is asleep, there is something in consciousness which declares that what then presents itself is but a dream." Kristen said as Akira rubbed his eyes.

"What?"

"Aristotle said that."

"Oh."

"I heard you gave Reiner a run for his money last night. I just read his full report. You're going to be an intermediate level shifter in no time."

Akira shrugged. He had mixed feelings. But she was right. With more practice, the stronger he would become.

"He thinks if you launched a fireball back in May when you started dream shifting you would have passed out right away. That's how much stronger you've become. Just remember you must discipline your spirit and your soul in order to become even more powerful. Think of it like training your body to wake up at the same time every morning, the more you do it the better you'll get."

Kind of like sex Akira thought.

"Anyway, let's get you back to school. You probably have a lot of homework to catch up on. Just remember 'excellent sleep is not an act, but a habit.'"

"Aristotle?"

Kristen only smiled back.

. . .

Kristen drove Akira home. He talked to her about his two fights. He was zero and two. That sucked.

He fumbled around with the thumb drive in his hand. He would make sure he wouldn't lose it. When Akira arrived back at school he told Ray to lay off Corey, and he received an ominous text from Sid: "I see you're back in town. Meet me at the Starbucks across from school at 2."

"What a creep." Akira thought as he prepared himself to go anyway.

At Starbucks Sid was sitting there with a laptop and a coffee. He was wearing an all-white hoodie. He looked up at Akira and smiled. "AY. Just the kid I was looking for."

Akira rolled his eyes. "Yeah, I know. Cause you texted me."

He closed his laptop.

"You're a member of the MLK now aren't you?"

Akira said nothing, but his face answered the question easy enough.

"It's even easier to sense you. You're like a torch in a blackout. Something's changed. I bet you've awakened your power."

Akira was impressed. "Wow, you can tell that just from sensing me?"

Sid nodded his head. "I bet you want to learn how to hide that power."

"Yeah, as a matter of fact," he looked keenly into Sid's eyes as he leaned forward. "I would."

Sid held up his pointer finger.

"First, you tell me if they gave you anything special. Secondly, tell me where their HQ is. They have some kind of system that keeps all of their energies suppressed or hidden."

Akira's face scrunched up. "Are you serious? You want me to betray them already? What do you care anyhow?"

Sid tapped his fingers together. "I like to be up to date with my adversaries. How about we make a wager? Me verse you?"

Thinking about it, Akira shook his head. It's too likely that Sid would win.

"I know something that even the MLK can't tell you. It's why they took a special interest in you."

Akira grimaced. "No more special than anyone else. It's just because I'm a Dream Shifter with potential." he said, almost trying to convince himself.

Sid had a devious smile.

What does he know that I don't?

"I'm leaving,"

Sid Meyers showed his teeth in an eager smile.

"Don't forget about the next Robotics meeting this Wednesday!"

"Whatever." Akira chimed while he got up abruptly and left.

Sid watched him go. *He'll give in eventually* Sid decided, then he turned his laptop back on and began typing away.

· · ·

SIX DAYS LATER. FRIDAY.
Ray got into a taxi. "Follow that black SUV."

"Excuse me?" The cab driver said turning. Ray handed him a twenty. The cab driver raised an eyebrow and Ray nodded towards the windshield. The driver sighed, took the money and pulled away from the curb and began following the SUV.

Ray handed him a five. "This will be for your discretion. Stay two to three cars back."

"You got it boss."

Fifty-two minutes and one extra bribe later, Ray was in Newark, New Jersey. He also urged the cab to stay even further back, because a New York cab on a Jersey freeway tends to stick out like nobody's business.

He paid the fare and walked across a street. He climbed up a dumpster and grabbed onto the roof of a small one story building. After climbing up, Ray took out binoculars from his backpack, and began watching the SUV. One block away, it went into a driveway that went downwards out of his line of sight. Ray jumped to the building next to him, and then once more to a third. He arrived just in time to see the garage door closing. Using his binoculars, he read a sign. **DOCTOR ABHI AHMAD M.D.** under that read: **SLEEP AID THERAPY**. He scribbled the information onto a notepad.

. . .

It was four in the afternoon. Philip Anthony Stone couldn't deal with his alter ego the night before, so he got blackout drunk. He woke up, excreted his waste, puked in the same toilet seconds later, flushed, and went back to sleep. Kenneth told him that he was filthy and he should shower. Philip argued that it was a motel, so it *had to be clean.*

In his dreams, Philip was still inebriated. He is sitting on a bench in his hometown Portsmouth, Virginia. Philip and Kenneth both agreed after Philip was arrested for the double-homicide of his brother and his girlfriend to never come back. However, Philip came here in his dreams; and in his dreams Kenneth was gone.

While Philip pet a massive, perhaps overly sized Golden Retriever, he was not thinking of the stress of life and living with the guilt he carried with him. Beside him was a brown paper bag that contained a bottle that he drank out of to forget the past.

It all happened when Philip was eighteen. Just old enough to be tried as an adult. Even back then Philip was diagnosed with bipolar disorder and very mild autism. Kenneth was never a diagnosed issue because he did not exist yet; at least not inside of Philip's head that is. When Philip got home from college, he found his dad and brother fighting. His brother gave his dad a shove, and as fate would have it, he snapped his neck on the end of a table. Philip went after Kenneth Stone with utter contempt and blind rage. Ken was two years older, but he couldn't compete with Phillip's natural strength. His girlfriend tried intervening, or one might say helping Kenneth rather than stopping the fight.

By the time his mom came home, Philip was hugging his dad's corpse and crying. Beside him was the bloody pulp of her other son and his late girlfriend. She testified on Philip's behalf. Philip's lawyers used the "Heat of the moment" defense. He received fifteen years of mandatory stay in a mental hospital. Three years later his mom committed suicide. Philip was only out of the hospital for two weeks before **The Dark Man** started harassing him.

The lush fur of the Golden Retriever was the most comforting thing around. Certainly more comforting than the burning forget-the-past solution that was in the bag beside him. Sometimes a lady would visit the hospital with several dogs. The good patients could pet the dogs. Philip was always on his best behavior so he could pet them. The dog was like a mobile pillow. "One day, I'm going to travel with a doggy just like you."

"You still have some travelling to do, comrade."

Philip looked around and saw nothing out of the ordinary. Then all of the cars and people around him stopped. They froze, like a picture. The Retriever started looking around as well. It began growling and baring it's teeth. "No. Nooo. Nice doggy. It's okay."

Philip's eyes expanded in horror when the dog caught on fire out of nowhere. It was a black flame. The poor pup began whimpering and howling in pain. **The Dark Man** was near. Philip started trying to put out the fire, but only managed to burn himself. The dog was yelping until all that was left was a tear in Phil's eye that dropped and splashed next to the pile of crisp ashes. It smelled awful.

The Dark Man was in front of him now. "You might be next. You're not done yet Philip. Don't make me tell everyone what you did. I'll tell the dogs, the people that serve your food, I'll tell your aunt Rose that you want to live with, I'll tell *everyone.*" The voice was coming from all around him. All of the faces around him became that of the Asian kid. Akira Kishimoto's face was plastered onto the face of the men and women frozen in their imagined daily urban interactions. Then a singeing noise was made as letters were scorched into the concrete in front of Philip's bench.

2067 East Main Street, Newark, New Jersey. Pain tore into Philip's left arm. Blood dripped onto his legs as he stared at his left arm. A bloody cut across his forearm read 2067 East Main Street, Newark, New Jersey. The blood was warm as it dripped down his arm. Philip screamed.

. . .

Akira was sitting in on his first MLK meeting. He only knew about half of the people in the room this time. Almost every seat was filled. He sat next to Reiner and Kristen.

"So, using the subconscious manipulation method, I managed to retrieve the briefcase carried by our late second-in-command Sean Singer. The police were unable to open the briefcase, but ultimately found it useless in a case where murder wasn't intentional. Without any known family to send the briefcase to, it remained untouched in an evidence locker. Gizmo, I want you to look into it. The lock is digitized, and I believe you helped Sean create the passcode."

A tall and chunky girl with unkempt brown hair spoke up. "Yeah boss, but I only know about half of what his code was. We set that shiddup to be impenetrable."

"I trust you can figure it out. I won't let Sean's sacrifice go in vain."

Jack stared at her fiercely and she looked down and twirled her thumbs.

"Got it Kilimanjaro."

Akira noted how much Jack liked the code names in these meetings, although he wasn't sure why. He was also surprised Jack's glare didn't shatter her glasses.

"Finally, I'd like to introduce the rest of you to our newest novice, Akira Kishimoto. Codename: Firebird."

Akira smiled. It was an improvement. He turned in his chair to acknowledge the rest of the members. Todd was still staring at his phone, like he was presumably doing during the whole meeting.

Abhi Ahmad was in full doctor garb. He gave Akira a nod. Next to him was the pretty and quiet girl Kara Summers. She looked at him but said and did nothing. Next to her was the nerdy looking girl who was not surprisingly named Gizmo. "Yo Noob. I'm Gizmo, or Joan. Whichever works. I'm the tech specialist here."

Akira shrugged. "Yeah, I figured." He let out an awkward laugh. "Nice to meet you."

Next to Joan was an empty seat. Next to that seat was an older Italian looking man with hair slicked back. He had a large cross and several rings on his fingers.

"My name is Jailbreak. Or you can call me Richie. That's all you need to know kid."

Akira nodded. And finally the last new face was a bearded man with glasses and two sleeves of tattoos not unlike Jack's.

"I am the Professor. I keep records of everything that the MLK is interested in and I'm the lead researcher as to why we have our powers. It's still a work in progress. Nice to meet you."

Akira reached over and shook the man's hand since he was in reach. Todd was leaning against his usual spot looking at his phone.

"Okay. Enough with the meet and greet. Akira. You and I are going to take a drive. Everyone else, you know what to do. Gizmo, your mission is top priority."

Everyone got up from their seats. Jack spun his car keys in his fingers.

"Let's go."

"You've got it." Akira answered. He was ready for whatever the boss man had to throw at him.

CHAPTER 25

JACK WAS DRIVING A BLACK sports car on the freeway. He weaved in and out of traffic. Akira noted the signs were saying they were headed east, towards New York. "So, what do you think of our little operation kid?" Jack asked, then lit a cigarette and opened the car window. He slowed down as the traffic got increasingly congested. Akira was looking at tattoo of a bomb from one of the old Mario games. It was a Bob-omb. On the underside of Jack's arm was a red dragon wrapped around a volcano that looked anything but dormant. There were other parts of Jack's sleeve Akira wanted to see, but couldn't.

"It's a neat little operation, that's for sure. Although, I'm still a little confused on some things."

"They'll be answered in due time. For now, you just need to know that we cure people of sleep paralysis and insomnia up in that doctor's office. But down below, we keep society safe."

He exhaled cigarette smoke. Akira loathed the smell. Some of it was pulled outside of the car, but the rest hit the steering wheel and spread out inside. It lingered invisibly. The putrid smell hung there, seemingly taunting Akira with its presence.

"Who is The Dark Man? I was so shocked by seeing someone else I know with powers, I forgot to ask Kristen."

Jack shook his head in disgust. "It's interesting how everyone silently calls him that in their heads. His real name is Dmitri Noskov. We don't know much about him, other than that he was born in Russia and.." Jack looked over and made quick eye contact with Akira. "And he was the very first Dream Shifter."

His eyes darted back to the road and he took another puff of his cigarette.

"Marco Peterson our founder, Dmitri Noskov, this guy named Elijah who was killed in battle, and the guy we're on our way to meet. All first generation Dream Shifters."

"Wow. So we're on our way to meet someone powerful?"

Jack nodded his head. Akira found himself staring at Jack's biceps in pure admiration. He started working out at the MLK gym and he already saw some progress, but he didn't think Jack missed a day. Then Akira decided it was time to stop looking at Jack in admiration, so he looked out the window at the passing scenery.

"Yep. The first ever rogue Dream Shifter. This guy took no alignment when Marco and Dmitri got into a power dispute."

More interested in The Dark Man than the man they were on their way to meet, Akira asked "So if Marco founded the MLK, what has Dmitri been doing for the last twenty-two years?"

"Once the MLK was formed, we foiled a plan he put in place to take over the local government in his hometown. It was before my time, but after that he remained low and hidden. After that he tried robbing a bank in Germany. He succeeded, but we were still there as a nuisance to him. After the MLK proved they wouldn't let him do what he wanted twice, he changed his plans. From 2008-2015 three of our members including the man that inducted me into the MLK and Marco himself, were murdered. Although one of those was technically a suicide. One other agent disappeared and is presumed dead. Since then, we have relocated and actively been more secretive. Unfortunately, we still couldn't track him down. Then in the last year, our losses were worse than ever as Kristen must have told you."

They were beginning to enter the Holland Tunnel. Darkness swallowed them. Then every other second the tunnel lights flashed over them. It made Jack look extra serious.

"Dmitri needs to be stopped. He's a psychopath and a murderer. And an intelligent one at that, which makes him all the more dangerous."

"I agree. But why am I going with you to meet this rogue?"

"That question will answer itself in a matter of minutes."

"Did you purposely lead me to a dead end? When I was first supposed to meet with Kristen?"

Jack produced a smirk. "No," he said. "Kristen did."

Akira doubted that, and Jack must have sensed it.

"She deals with potential inductees at her own discretion. In your case she wanted to make sure you had survival skills and a strong enough will to live. It appears you passed."

"That's a load of B.S. I could have died!"

"Don't you know that the same is true for every mission in the MLK? This is no day care kid. If you think her methods are too harsh, take it up with her. But I support it fully, we have the best intentions and only the best of us can become field agents. So stop whining and start thinkin' about how and why you got out of there. That won't be the only time you'll be caught in a corner, and that, I promise you."

Akira stared at Jack, but said nothing. There was nothing to say. After a while, Jack spoke up again.

"What is the one thing they fail to teach you in school?"

"Anything useful?" Akira answered sardonically.

"A half-truth for sure, but not what I mean. The answer is patience. Think back to High School. Did they ever force patience upon you? Children are naturally impatient. Perhaps waiting for lunch is the closest they came to doing so. Look around you. Americans especially are an impatient people. They are rash, ignorant, and ready to jump on anything or anyone without thinking. Impatience causes more accidents a year than alcohol. People hardly even have the patience to sit down and read a book anymore; yet patience will get you everywhere in life."

Akira considered this. He watched cars cut each other off. Honk at one another. Nearly run down pedestrians. But he also thought back to Jack weaving in and out of traffic not even half an hour ago.

"The time for my patience is done. I've waited my due and watched friends die. Dmitri will pay. But for you, being patient is still important. Be patient with pain, love, and fear..it's all you can do sometimes. Remember, nothing in the world lasts forever. The universe just isn't built that way."

· · ·

Gizmo drank from her mug of coffee. She was delighted with herself. She just cracked the code to the briefcase. She did what the police techs could not do, and it felt damn good. *I wonder if Jack wants me to look inside Sean Singer's briefcase then contact him. He wasn't too clear about that.* Gizmo was thinking about how happy she was to be useful, but she wasn't thinking about the dream from last night that evaded her memory. The Dark Man did not forget. He was in New York City now. And he could not sense the MLK in their protective base. But he could sense that the strongest shifter left the base with the kid.

Jack Ryder thought he was worthy of filling in Marco Peterson's shoes. Dmitri disagreed. Jack's ability to conceal their powers was impressive, but when Dmitri was so close it mattered not. He had, after all, been doing this longer than Jack Ryder had been alive. When Gizmo flew in on a plane from Atlanta he had tracked her. He invaded her dreams on the plane. To dream shift into a passenger travelling so fast, is a near impossible feat. No one in the MLK even dreamed of attempting it. Yet Dmitri had defeated Gizmo in a shifter battle with ease nonetheless.

Instead of trapping her inside herself, he wiped her memory of the encounter and left some of his dark energy inside of her. For two days the energy festered and waited to be unleashed. Now she was a puppet of his will. He was unsure for how long because of the brain wave barrier that Jack had likely built, but he assumed it would be long enough.

Dmitri pulled an invisible tether and Gizmo's pupils went from brown to a dull gray. Her hands let go of her phone and mug simultaneously. The mug plopped onto the desk two inches below spilling coffee on the desk and briefcase. Her phone dropped into her lap uselessly. She walked over to the security center that Akira has not yet seen. She typed in her access code. Ignoring the security monitors in the room, she went over to a console and typed in her access code once more.

Typing away a storm, she unlocked the garage access and the stairwell access points. Dmitri did not know of these things except through her own prior knowledge. "Two more chores for you my dear." He said out loud in his fancy hotel room eighteen stories high in New York, only several blocks away from Jack and Akira. His eyes were closed but maintained a faint blackish glow through his eyelids.

Joan deactivated the on-base alarms and recalculated the brain wave blocking technology to also block radio waves. This prevented any outgoing calls. Then she unplugged the router and smashed it with her foot. No more internet either. "Good job, my darling piglet."

Dmitri said as he severed the communication. He was unsure what would happen to her when he did that (it varied) and he did not care.

Gizmo collapsed immediately in the security room behind the closed door. She was hardly breathing anymore.

Meanwhile, three men in hockey masks were across the street in an alleyway. One of them was in a full cop uniform. The other was wearing a Starbucks apron. The third was wearing raggedy clothes almost a week old and kept talking to himself. He held a 9MM pistol in his hands. The police officer held a .357 Magnum in his. The Starbucks barista had military grade explosives in a backpack he wore, and a baseball bat.

"Philip. Ze time iz now. Do what you must und you will forever be free of your guilt, and ov me. You need not worry about ze Asian boy any longer, he'll be dealt with."

"Yes Darkman. I understand."

All we have to do is commit more murder and we're done you halfwit idiot.

"I'm glad that horrible Asian boy won't be inside there. He's truly a monster. Almost as bad as the Darkman himself."

Shaddup and get those mind zombies to follow us.

Kenneth and Philip had agreed they would move away to where the Darkman couldn't reach them after this. They would get a dog and be done with everything. Philip was licking his teeth in excitement beneath the hockey mask.

"Let's go."

The duo with dull grey eyes peering out of their masks followed Philip Anthony Stone without saying a word.

CHAPTER 26

AKIRA WATCHED JACK NAVIGATE THROUGH the city streets with one hand on the steering wheel. He drove with the confidence of a cab driver and the precision of a police officer.

"You grew up here didn't you?" Akira asked.

Jack grew a half-grin on his face.

"I guess it takes a New Yorker to know one eh?"

He flicked his cigarette out the window.

They pulled into a parking garage. Jack paid the toll for two hours. They parked on the third floor and walked down. Next to the garage was a Hotel.

They entered and slipped past the clerk.

The duo entered an elevator and Akira watched Jack hit the button for the fifteenth floor. Next to the button was **PS**.

The doors slid open and a hotel worker with a utility cart loaded with suitcases waited for them to exit before entering. After a minute of passing identical looking hotel rooms, they got up to room **1506**. Jack rapped on the door three times. The door opened. Jack and Akira walked in. It was a presidential suite. Akira noted that it was bigger than his old apartment. The figure with dark hair and a blue buttoned down shirt walked away from them and led them to three chairs. Then he turned around and Akira saw his face.

Horror dawned on him. It was the last person on Earth that he wanted to see.

• • •

Philip Stone walked to the doctor's office. The door was locked. The office was closed. Philip Anthony Stone would not be deterred by a lock. He smashed the handle off with the butt of the gun and kicked the door open. The lights were off and the sun had just set. The office was swallowed by a dangerous darkness. A dim light was on at the end of the hallway though. Philip walked towards it.

Shoot them all. Kill them all dead. But remember, we've got seven bullets in here, try not to dump them all into one guy.

Philip knew that this mission required stealth, so he did not respond to Kenneth. He leaned his back against the wall next to the half open door that read **DR. ABHI AHMAD M.D.**

He pushed the door open with one hand without looking in the room.

"Hello? Anyone there?" Inquired the brown doctor.

Philip heard him get up and knew he had to act. He turned into the doorway and fired a shot. It clipped the shoulder and the bearded man recoiled.

The brown doctor gave a loud grunt in pain but began charging. He tried grabbing the gun from Philip who responded by punching him in the face, sending the brown doctor's glasses flying. The doctor turned the gun again and Philip depressed the trigger again. The shot went into the doctor's foot, who loosened his grip on the handgun. Philip kicked him and he went over his desk and flipped over. He left a trail of blood from where he confronted Philip to the desk he flipped over. Now you could only see his foot hanging on the edge of the desk. His shoe was already soaked in red.

Leave him to bleed out for now. We have to go in case someone else heard-shit-

As Phil turned a small blonde girl punched him in the stomach and roundhouse kicked his hand holding the gun. He threw a punch and she blocked it with her small hands. She fired off a kick that connected with Philip's testicles. He crumpled into a hunch as the pain exploded throughout his groin.

. . .

Gary Waller was a cop for seven years when Dmitri invaded his dreams to use him as a puppet the next day. There was no specific reason why Dmitri chose Gary. He just had access to a gun and confiscated explosives, and Dmitri sensed he would be more effortless to manipulate than other officers might be. So here he was with Jacob Mars who walked out of his job mid-shift when Dmitri took over. They entered the access code to the garage, and it opened. There were two black sedans, a black SUV, a motorcycle and space for about two other cars. They walked around them with indifference.

Curiously enough, Gary began using the cars as cover, perhaps through instincts embedded in him from training, but Jacob simply waltzed in between the black motor vehicles. As Gary opened the unlocked door to the base, two muted bangs were heard. They didn't sound like gunshots, but a veteran of weapons training or anyone who's lived next to train tracks or the inner-city projects will know that is the sound of a muffled handgun discharging. They opened the door and Richard Muchiani was walking towards them.

"What the fuck?"

Gary Waller fired one blast from the massive .357 Magnum and it sent Richie "Jailbreak" Muchiani fluttering backward. The bullet penetrated his rib cage with ease. Gary continued inside. Jacob entered behind him, baseball bat in hand. He looked at the body of Richie to make sure he was dead. Then he followed Gary who was also drowning in a sea of apathy. Gary held his magnum in both hands as he entered the kitchen. The fridge door was wide open, partially hiding Gizmo. They could almost smell her sweat. He kicked the door and it smacked into her face and opened again. She fell onto her butt.

"I don't know who you are but please don't kill me. PLEASE." she pleaded.

Gizmo did not know that only moments ago she was a mind slave just like them. She thought she fell asleep and woke up hungry. She was also unaware that her begging fell on deaf ears. Gary slowly raised the revolver about an inch upwards until it was aligned with her face. Joan was crying through closed eyes. The hand cannon fired. The devastation to her face was immense at such a close range. The exit wound on the back of her head actually allowed you to see the reddened wall behind her. Her body fell, crumpled amongst her own skull fragments and the remnants of her brain.

Jacob wasted no time to charge into the next room. He ran at the man in the wheelchair and swung this bat like an axe over his head. The wheelchair guy went in reverse and then stopped the chair, and sped back towards Jacob. He swung the bat at the same time the wheelchair man launched himself off of the chair. His limp weight brought both of them down to the ground.

Now Reiner unleashed a fury of punches onto Jacob. Within fifteen seconds Jacob had a broken nose and lost two teeth.

Gary came into the meeting room and fired two shots at Reiner. The first hit him in the upper chest by the shoulder and propelled

Reiner off of his mindless counterpart. The second shot punched a baseball sized hole in one of the chairs. It instantly collapsed.

Gary quietly took stock of how many shots he fired. It was an eight shot clip. He did not bring extra ammo with him. He walked over to Reiner who was holding his considerable wound, and aimed the gun at his head. Reiner's eyes were angry yet accepting. *Everyone has their time,* he thought in German in his own head.

· · ·

Philip looked back up as tears welled up in his eyes. Suddenly the blonde girl was Kenneth Stone's girlfriend Claire. The one who called him a "freak" and a "retard" as she was throwing stuff at him and trying to claw his eyes.

The girl was about to go for his gun, but when he looked at her, she saw something different in his eyes. Something changed. She saw a look that she wanted to unsee. It was the same look her father had when he beat her. Utter contempt. Unmistakable rage. The kind that has no regrets. Kara backed away. Neither of them paid attention to the first two bangs from the louder and more powerful .357 magnum downstairs, which was followed by two more shots.

Philip charged at her and she threw the door into his face. He shoulder checked it and the top two hinges came off. The impact tipped the door over onto her. Then he jump kicked it and the last hinge broke off.

The broken door on top of her hurt, but when Philip jumped on it she truly felt like she was going to die. Compressed and in pain, she couldn't move. Philip fired a bullet into the door he stood on. The wood splintered and shot out, and he thought the bullet might have ricocheted but he was unsure. Kenneth told him to keep moving and he did. He fired another shot into the wooden door beneath him. He noted to come back upstairs and make sure they were both dead after he was done. He opened the door to the stairwell, and went to meet up with Dmitri's mind slaves.

In the deep recesses of Philip's mind, he knew that he wasn't going to be okay. His double homicide has now been doubled. He was going to end up in jail, or dead. He went too far this time. But any of those options were better than another visit from **The Dark Man**. He wished in the back of his mind he could play with another fluffy dog one more time.

· · ·

Gary was aiming his firearm at Reiner's head when something hit his gun as he fired. The bullet impacted the floor two inches from Reiner's head. Gary's puppet reflexes were apparently stronger than his police training, because he looked for the object instead of the suspect. When he realized it was a cell phone thrown at a high speed, he looked up just in time to see Todd Rimando jam a pocket knife into his stomach. The mind puppet was immune to the sensation of pain, as Todd found out when Gary began to calmly re-aim his magnum at Todd.

Todd let go of the knife, and he blocked the gun hand as it rotated towards him. Then he grabbed the gun and seized control of Gary's palm with his free hand and twisted it up and over himself to avoid having his face in the line of fire. This turned Gary around. Then Gary's grip on the gun loosened from pressure and Todd took control of it turning it on Gary. The gun was aimed at the back of Gary's head while Todd maintained a grip on the twisted arm.

"NO DON'T!" Kristen was holding an emergency medical kit. Her eyes were darting from the unarmed cop in a hockey mask to Reiner slowly bleeding out on the floor.

"He's innocent Todd."

"This man just killed two of our friends." Todd answered with undisguised anger.

"He's not in control of his actions. You can see it in his eyes." she pleaded.

Then Jacob started to get back up. Just as he scooped up the cold wooden baseball bat, Todd detected his motion peripherally and blew Gary's head apart. He aimed it at Jacob but Jacob moved so the headless corpse of Gary was in between them. Todd used his arm to assist the body in falling to the ground faster and Jacob swung the bat. It hit the gun right when it fired. Jacob's left arm that swung the bat collapsed but he swung it with his other hand hitting Todd in the side. Todd suffered through the pain and used his elbow to hold the bat in place while he kicked Jacob back. Jacob fell on top of the corpse of the late Gary.

Todd stepped over and swung the baseball bat hard into Jacob's head. This effectively knocked him out. The tip of the bat looked like a brush dipped in red paint.

Kristen wasted no time to run over to Reiner.

"We need to get him to a hospital now or he won't make it."

"Shit. This is so fucked." Todd said.

He was thinking about what they were going to do with all of these dead bodies. How would they explain gunshot wounds to doctors and inquisitive police? He opened the backpack Jacob was wearing after he tied his hands behind his back.

"Kristen."

She was wrapping Reiner's wound to stop the bleeding.

"Yeah?" she responded without looking up.

"There are explosives in here.."

• • •

The Professor heard the gunshots and was more terrified than he thought he could be in a dangerous situation. When he heard the first one he brushed off the impossibility of a live firearm in the base discharging. Then he heard another. And another. He thought to himself he should make sure the others were okay. But the gunshots sounded like they were coming from upstairs too. As soon as his brain deduced the possibility of an enemy intelligent or tactical enough to attack from both entrances, his fear became terror.

He had a girlfriend. A mom. A dad. One day he wanted to have children. It was fight or flight for him. He needed to survive. Then he heard the doors in the hallway getting kicked in. One. Then another. Then one more. Then it stopped. The Professor imagined that they didn't want to announce their presence any more than they had to. He imagined a SWAT team sized group of armed soldiers. And yet, when they kicked the door open and he hid behind the bed furthest from the door---his bed, he stopped sweating.

You fucking coward, he told himself in a whisper.

The Professor remembered the trust Jack put in him. He didn't want to let him down, but more importantly, how could he live with himself if he let all of his friends die? The metaphoric blood would be on his hands, and he knew he would drown in it. After a moment, he turned and saw the room was empty. The door was wide open unlike before. The assailant had moved on.

• • •

"Don't fucking move or I shoot."

Philip Anthony Stone held the 9mm pistol fiercely. It was aimed at Kristen. Todd knew the safety was off. He knew he couldn't risk Kristen's life like he could his own. Philip knew it too. Kenneth had told him right away.

"Drop the gun Blue Hair."

Todd placed the gun on the floor.

I don't like his eyes Phil. I don't like them one bit. He's killing us in his mind. I can see it Phil. Shoot him then the girl. Those blue eyes are stabbing at us Phil. DO IT.

Philip Stone raised the gun to aim at Todd. Todd closed his eyes and bent his knees a little bit. The likelihood of dodging a bullet was just about impossible. But maybe he might miss. Or he might miss a vital organ. Anything was better than letting the psycho execute everyone in the room.

"Your eyes aren't like the other two. You're in control aren't you?"

Philip's eyebrows lifted up to his forehead and his nose twitched.

"You have no remorse. You're a monster."

Philip read something like that once. It was in an old newspaper. **"Single mother kills herself after monster-of-a-son butchers entire family,"** it had said.

He lowered the gun just a little and screamed.

"YOU SON OF A BITCH THE DARK MAN WILL DEVOUR YOU. HE'LL DEVOUR US ALL TO GET WHAT HE WANTS!"

As soon as he started screaming Todd began moving. He was quicker than Philip anticipated. He continued screaming while he followed Todd with the barrel of the gun. Philip's second of hesitation had cost him his clear shot. Everything was in slow motion. His fear of missing overcame him. He stopped following Todd's sprint. He brought the gun back towards the beautiful woman next to the bleeding man. His face contorted into a twist of rage and insanity.

Todd yelled something. Kristen looked the 9mm pistol down it's barrel. She wondered if she'd be able to see the bullet when it was fired.

Then, the lights went out.

PART V

DMITRI & AKIRA

...

CHAPTER 27

"HELLO SON," THE WELL-DRESSED MAN facing Akira said. His face was neither happy nor sad.

Akira's was a caricature of horror. He looked at Jack who only bit his lower lip and looked down.

"What's going on here.. why are you.. Jack? What's-" He was tripping over his words. He was also dimly aware that he began shaking.

"I think it might be best if you took a seat Akira,"

He pulled out a one-person couch.

"We have a lot to talk about."

At this point in time, Dmitri's three puppets had just entered the MLK base. There were two attempts to contact Jack and one attempt to call an ambulance. All failed. Their signals failed them. Their base cut them off from the outside world.

Akira's dad was drinking coffee. He gave a cup to Jack as well, but Akira refused. Yakashi Kishimoto was engaged in small talk until Akira interrupted it.

"So how long have you been in New York *dad*? If I can even call you that."

He looked like Akira's sarcastic pronunciation of *dad* slapped him in the face but he answered nonetheless.

"Only about a week. I assumed that the MLK was tracking me, so I figured if I flew to America they would find me."

"I had a feeling you wanted to be found." Jack said.

"Well it saved me the trouble of having to find you guys." he chuckled.

"So wait a minute. You're the rogue Dream Shifter..?"

Akira's dad stared intently into his eyes.

"Yes. I was there were Marco founded the MLK. I was his first member. We both agreed my former teacher was out of hand and a threat."

"The Dark Man? You learned from..him?"

"Yes. Dmitri Noskov taught me how to use my powers. He wouldn't tell me how long he had his powers, but I knew it was longer than me."

"So why did you leave?"

"I got married. I told Marco twenty years ago in 2000 that I wasn't going to use my powers anymore, I just wanted to be with my wife. We had a falling out. Two years later you were born."

"And then you left me and mom to fend for ourselves."

"I left to protect you two. Dmitri knew how much of a threat I was to him. I couldn't put you guys at risk. Eight years after that in 2008 I moved back to Japan. People in the MLK were dropping dead. Marco himself was put in a coma that year."

There was visible water in his eyes. Akira hated him. But he couldn't help the water coming to his own eyes. *Like father like son.*

"But you told her it was because you didn't love her. You said you cheated on her!"

"Akira. I never told her about the powers. I lied about my past. I lied about everything. I didn't even cheat. I ruined everything.

She's dead because of me. I still love her and she's dead because of ME." He slammed his fist into the wall.

A single tear streamed down his face and got caught in his goatee.

"What were you doing in Japan? Why would you run away and not do anything?"

"At first I thought getting away was good enough. So all I did was find a livable job. I obtained a mild cocaine addiction. I traded that for an alcohol addiction a year later. Booze is cheaper after all. More members of the MLK disappeared. I couldn't stand idly by anymore. I was done being useless and wasting away while monitoring MLK channels. After that I kicked my addictions and focused on improving my powers so I could take Dmitri Noskov down and return back to my family. Your mom and I were alike in that way, neither of us ever settled down with anyone again. I overcame addictions that plagued me for the two of you."

"She certainly tried to. I urged her to find someone too. And I don't care if you do more coke than Lindsey Lohan, you left us."

Yakashi gave an understanding frown.

"He put her in that coma. He killed her. I'm going to make him pay. But I can't do it without you. Akira. You're the first case where powers have been passed down to the next generation. We think that gives you extra potential. Potential to become the next leader of the MLK. In my solitude, I learned a technique that only Dmitri and I can do." he said and wiped his eyes.

"Son. I can give you my powers. Permanently."

Akira stood up.

"I DON'T WANT ANYTHING FROM YOU EVER AGAIN, YOU'VE ALREADY DONE ENOUGH." He flipped the couch on its side then stormed out of the room.

"Akira wait!" Jack called after him.

"Give him time," Yakashi said, already facing the glass wall of a window. He was staring at the city. The lights calmed him, but he missed the cities of Japan. He missed his innocent son; so happy and curious. Almost completely free of the hatred and violence of the world.

"He's driven by emotion. He's a sensitive boy, but an intelligent one. I know Akira will come to. The boy wants to avenge his mother and do what's right."

"You seem to know him well despite your absence from his life."

Ignoring the query, Yakashi said "I'll follow him. Go back to your HQ. I feel something pretty weird. Almost like an active shifter in the city is doing something, but I can't read a connection and it's making me uneasy. Go check on your people Jack Ryder."

Jack doubted that Dmitri could have found their secret base. He personally slaved over making it as non-descript as possible. Everything he did was to maintain the security of the hidden base. But still, Jack was not one to take any chances. Especially after no one was answering the downstairs or the upstairs phones.

Akira came out of the elevator bawling. His tears made his cheeks shine. He didn't care what the hotel patrons and workers thought. He knew that he needed to get as far away from his dad as possible. As he ran past the parking garage him and Jack entered in, he guessed he needed to get away from the MLK and the importance and sacrifices that came with having supernatural powers. Akira knew he was in a form of denial, but again, he didn't care. He just wanted to pretend things were okay. He wanted to pretend the apartment he grew up in with his mom wasn't being occupied by total strangers, he wanted to pretend that he smoked weed and drank for fun with his best friends Cody and Jake and Cooper, not to escape (Amy). (Mom). (Life).

He was at the end of the block. He reached into his pocket and took out his ancient iPod Classic. He put on a playlist specifically for when he feels low. Then he turned and saw his dad watching him from the entrance to the hotel. *GET AWAY FROM ME* Akira thought but did not scream.

He ran as soon as the street was clear. Light snow flurries began to fall. They were only visible under streetlights and in front of the headlights of the congested city streets. He didn't know where he was going. Back to school maybe? But then he saw a sign about Penn Station. He texted Cody.

"Can you pick me up from Ronkonkoma Station? I'm going to take the train home."

Cody happily complied.

CHAPTER 28

AKIRA GOT IN CODY'S CAR. They hugged and said they loved and missed each other. There was never a need to say "no homo" after. The heterosexual duo was not embarrassed by their friendship on any level and neither of them were homophobic or uncomfortable with themselves. Akira wanted to tell Cody everything, but he decided to bear that burden himself. Instead, he told Cody that school was rough and his dad made a point to be in his life again.

"Man. Let's grab something to eat alright? We need to you to be positive homie." Cody said.

"Yeah that sounds nice. I get extra emotional and dramatic when I'm hungry." Akira said. He was feeling a little bit better already.

• • •

When the lights flashed back on Philip saw that his shot missed the girl. Then he saw blackness and his body collapsed forwards. The Professor stood behind Philip with a lead pipe. Philip's hand started reaching for the gun and The Professor hit him in the head again. Then he kicked the gun away.

"I have a good friend that's a doctor. I already went outside and texted him. I told him it's serious. We can trust him. I'm so happy I made it back down in time."

"Why am I tied up? Who are you people?" Jacob was looking around and beginning to cry. He wasn't the only one. Kristen joined him. "Thank God. Now we need to make sure everyone else is okay."

. . .

Akira enjoyed a nice hot meal with Cody. Cody was able to cheer him up more than he realized was possible. Akira was already cracking jokes and making references only Cody would understand left and right.

"I think it's time we get you a proper Long Island introduction."

Akira had a feeling he knew what Cody meant. And he was right. Cody invited about fifteen people into his basement. They drank and partied. Cody even paid for his parents to go out to eat. Then his and Jake's band played. A drunk Akira caught up with Angela while the band played. She told him she heard Amy and Jack broke up. Akira couldn't help but feel happy about that. He was in love with Amy and he wanted her to be happy, but at that moment he realized his selfishness. He wanted her to be happy with him. One of the girls at the party kept looking at him and smiling. She laughed at several of his mediocre jokes. Akira played dumb and he did not know why. Angela even came over and told him that the girl thought he was cute. He acted surprised. The party went on.

At 3 AM there were only five people left. Jake and Angela were in their room spooning. Cody and Cooper were smoking weed outside. Akira was passed out in his bed. He did not fall asleep thinking sad thoughts. His last thoughts were pleasant ones of how much he missed his bed and how happy he was that Cody and Jake weren't mad at him for his limited contact with them. That, and of course the inescapable notion that maybe he had a shot with Amy again. These inebriated thoughts passed quickly as he drifted off. Little did he know, his friends had just barely survived a massacre. Jack would try to call Akira, only to find that Akira let his phone die during another intoxicated ADD episode.

Yakashi Kishimoto was in a cheap motel about five miles away. He was typing up a storm on his laptop. It was a page and a half document titled: Akira.

That was when he sensed it. *Oh shit. Dmitri. This isn't good.* He began meditating.

Brent Armstrong, Tyler Walker and Ian Mckinley were driving together with a joint being passed around.

"Do you really believe that nutjob Brent?" asked Tyler from the backseat.

"It doesn't matter if he's crazy. His money is good. That's all I care about." Ian passed the joint back to Tyler.

"Yeah yeah yeah," spat Brent. "Win-win. You better be fucking careful Tyler. You saw *A Bronx Tale* right? If you do that I swear I'll kick your cock sucking ass in Hell."

Tyler looked at the box of molotov cocktails and then threw the joint out the window.

"Better safe than sorry."

"Shit, you owe me five bucks." Ian said.

They pulled up to the Portside Motel and each got out. Brent was holding onto a sledgehammer he grabbed from the trunk. Tyler was holding the crate with five explosive devices inside it.

"Let's go. Quick and easy." Ian said. Brent took out his phone. An unknown number texted the motel room number. Brent didn't know how he knew that, but he incorrectly guessed that the weirdo Russian hacked the motel's system. The motel didn't even have a system to be hacked. It only had one security camera, facing the office and the safe inside.

Brent swung the sledgehammer into the glass window shattering it entirely as soon as the massive hammer impacted the glass. Then Ian moved the curtains out of the way and grabbed two cocktails from the crate. Tyler lit the first one immediately and the second shortly after. Ian threw one directly onto the bed. He thought the Asian dude sitting there Indian style looked vaguely familiar. The cocktail slammed into the backboard of the motel bed he was sitting on, instantly shattering and exploding into hellish fire. The fire engulfed the bed almost im-mediately. It followed the booze everywhere it sprayed, devouring it in a hungry blaze. It swallowed the man, but Ian was freaked out when the man didn't move. He didn't even open his eyes.

Ian did as he was ordered and climbed out of the window while throwing another one at the floor in front of the window. Then he threw the other three at the door to block out escape. There was no other exit.

"Let's go. Go go go go."

The worker in the motel came out of the office just in time to see a third hooded figure run back to a car after committing his final arsonist act. There was an audible skid and the smell of rubber was strong as they peeled out of the parking lot. The employee ran back in and dialed 911. Tyler was the only one regretting the act they had just committed.

• • •

Her soft lips were on his. Their tongues touched and slid against each other like two swords in combat. He had already finished but he went until she was there too. When she let it be known that she was there by way of a moan turning into a light hum of the letter 'm' and the biting of her lower lip, Akira decided it was time to talk.

"So you and Jack?"

"It's complicated."

"I see. Then I guess we're done here then, aren't we?"

"Akira," Amy pleaded. Her beautiful brown eyes were staked into his own.

He looked away and she got off of him. She sat with her legs hanging off of the bed. "Listen Amy." Akira placed his hand on her shoulder but it suddenly felt very cold. "Amy?" He jumped out of the bed and put his hands on her cold cheek and turned her head to his.

Amy's skin was peeling off of her flesh. Her left eye was bleeding and her right was vacant. You could see the bone around it and it looked..cracked..faded. Akira fell backwards onto his ass. His eyes started watering.

"No. No no no. What's going on here?"

"Akira. Akira. Akira. Akirrrrrrraaaaaaaa."

Her mouth was barely moving. She stood up and staggered towards him.

"Please no Amy.. I can't lose you too. Not a third time. Please."

Her face contorted into a smile.

"You lost me a long time ago. And you knowwwwww ittttt."

"Akira." A new voice called his name. The Amy-like entity seemed shocked by it too. She twisted her one eye upwards and looked around.

"We don't have much time."

Yakashi Kishimoto materialized between them and the Amy look-alike screamed like a vampire caught in light and disintegrated. Akira was thankful to see it gone. Suddenly the dark room was gone. They were on top of a skyscraper somewhere Akira has never been. He had clothes on now. He got onto his feet and saw neon lights all over. "I'm dreaming. This is a dream."

"Akira I love you so much. More than words could ever express and if those are my dying words so be it. I have much to tell you, but my time is short, in both planes that is."

"I don't have anything to say to you."

Yakashi fell to one knee and grunted in pain. For a flash of a second his body was covered in reddish scars and burn marks, then he was back to normal.

Akira's hand was glowing blue again. "We need to do this now. When you wake up you're going to go to the local police station and get my laptop. I pray it is still salvageable.

"What are you talki-"

Yakashi walked over to him and grabbed his left hand turning it upwards.

"That blue symbol is the Japanese Kanji symbol for fire." It was a blue 'K' looking symbol with a dash behind it. 火 Then with his other hand he grabbed Akira's forehead. Now Yakashi's hand glowed blue.

"I am so sorry my son. I would take my own life a hundred times to bring your mother back." He cringed again in pain. "You will always have the power to control your own destiny. You're destined for greatness. Never let anyone tell you otherwise."

Akira couldn't explain why he wasn't feeling hatred anymore. It was something more of despair.

"Dad?"

"Aghghhh-ughhhheghhhhk" Yakashi's skin flashed back to a reddish black covered with blisters and then faded away. He was gone. Akira looked around at the empty rooftop. Then he saw him on the next rooftop over. It was the Dark Man. Dmitri Noskov was standing there with a trench coat flowing in the wind, staring at him.

What have you done? Akira's fist was clenched so hard his nails were digging into his palm tattoo.

CHAPTER 29

DMITRI NOSKOV LEVITATED OVER TO the building Akira was on. He was still hovering above it when he said: "I'm sorry my boy, it appears I have officially made you an orphan."

"LIAR!" Akira shot out a flare of fire from his left hand but Dmitri simply knocked it aside. It faded away a few feet from where he deflected it.

"At least you'll be more of a challenge now. I know I don't deserve it, but come join me. Be my apprentice as your fadder was twenty-five years ago."

Akira put his hands together behind the left side of his back and then launched a fireball. Then another. Dmitri swatted them away like flies.

"You have so much potential boy. I could really use you for the greater good."

"Greater good? You're a murderer!"

"Any man who truly loves humans, who loves the idea of what this world *could be*, is willing to dirty his hands for what he believes."

Dmitri's feet finally touched down on the building.

"And what is it that you believe?"

He tossed Akira a flashlight that came out of nowhere.

"Put this in your left hand boy."

He caught it. "I'm so sick of everyone referring to me as a child. In a few months I'll be nineteen. I don't view the world the way a kid does anymore."

"Zhat makes you all zhe more perfect. Zhis world is flawed. Money und hateful religion rule over all else. Politics control zhe people, not zhe other way around. Zhe democratic process iz garbage. Greedy little swine zhat are supposed to represent zhe people just follow zheir own personalized agendas of bias, hatred zand greed. Zhe media is supposed to expose criminals and show the truth, instead it's a petty product used to control zhe masses. Dis goes on in more countries than dees one. It's a global problem. I have not killed without purpose. I kill to stop zhe thousands of innocents zhat die every single day."

"Well I wouldn't know too much about that, but I do know it doesn't give you the right to kill. Besides, you *like* what you do." Akira said this defiantly. He put the flashlight in his left hand, but instead of light protruding out, a long blade-shaped flame took its place.

"Jew haven't seen what I've seen keed. Africa has hundreds dying every day because of corrupt governments letting terrorist cells you've never even heard of walk amongst their people freely. Zhe Middle East is always at war, constantly. Many have never known peace in the history of man. Entire generations know only hatred and bloodshed. The divide between Europe and The Middle East is only getting worse and worse. Climate change is slowly preparing to decimate nations. Entire countries and states will be underwater in a century or two and people only care about the now. Can't you feel it? Something big and bad iz going to happen soon. Best-case scenario, another foreign world leader gets assassinated and it's barely covered in Amerika. Worst- case scenario there's a nuclear war. It is my life's goal to stop this from getting worse. I will take over the world one government at time. One world leader at time. I'll start with the president, then China. I will rule this world. I will turn it into a sustainable world. Not for fame or fortune, but for the greater good. I will do it behind the scenes. The name Dmitri Noskov will not be remembered in the decades to come. Humans will foolishly think their leaders are to thank. I am okay with this.

"World peace will be achieved. That is why I have been given these powers. I will take out anyone that stands in my way. Any survivors of the MLK will fall tonight." Akira hardly recognized Dmitri's accent fade away.

"You're a fanatic and a lunatic. The people have to fix things themselves!"

Akira swung the blade of fire at him.

He disappeared and then reappeared with his hand on Akira's throat.

"You and I both know that won't happen."

• • •

Jack fell to his knees. He was crying. There were four corpses next to him. There were sheets covering them. Some red seeped through the white sheets. Other red blood escaped onto the carpet around the sheet. This was the worst day in his entire life and he had some pretty bad ones. He needed to try to call Akira again, but he couldn't focus on anything right now.

"I've failed everyone."

• • •

This time Akira placed his feet on Dmitri's chest and kicked off of it into a black flip. He took Dmitri's second of surprise as his advantage and came at him with the fire sword again as soon as he landed. Dmitri's sidestepped swipe after swipe, and then kicked at Akira's leg sending him off balance. Dmitri then grabbed Akira's wrist holding the sword and yanked him forward and Akira nearly fell onto his own weapon.

"I gave you this weapon to show ju jyour potential. The em-ell-kay will never bring out all of your power."

He sent a stab at Dmitri's chest and this time Dmitri didn't sidestep it, he blocked it with his open hand, dark-purple energy swirling around it. The flames at the tip of the sword seemingly fought against the purple energy.

"I don't care if I'm weak. I will stand by who is right."

"Jyou're too young to know who's right. Are jew so sure jew don't want ze power to avenge jyour deceased parents?"

"SHUT UP." Fire shot out from the blade engulfing Dmitri's arm. He quickly jumped ten feet backwards in one leap. He landed on the edge of the roof with his left arm still smoking. He was sick of Dmitri and his stupid accent.

"Jew claim I like what I do. You are not wrong. See, having dis much power iz maddening. It becomes so easy to became sadistic or apathetic. Join me and you will keep me sharp like an arrow. We will achieve world peace together. With me, you can literally change zhe world, can't you wrap your puny mind around dat, boy?"

. . .

Jack grabbed a chair with both of his hands and threw it into the TV in the meeting room. The TV regurgitated sparks and fell to the ground cackling. The large meeting table was pushed up against the wall. He went down the hallway. The Professor was blocking him. "Hey Jack, it's not your fault." Jack grabbed his shoulder and shoved him aside. "Out of my way Jerry." He kicked open the dorm room door and walked over to Philip Anthony Stone who was handcuffed to a bedframe. Todd was guarding him. Jack sent a kick into Philip's jaw. Todd and the Professor grabbed both of Jack's arms to hold him back.

"This fucking dick deserves to be dead." Jack said, knowing he could overpower both Todd and Jerry if he really wanted. Instead he was allowing them to restrain him because deep down he wanted to be calm and analytical instead of self-loathing and full of rage.

They had knocked Jacob out and Kristen and a wounded Abhi Ahmad used an advanced technique where they wiped his brain of the last twenty-four hours. When he woke up later, he was outside of his job on a bench with a killer hangover.

Kristen walked into the room. "We've tended to everyone that we could. Jerry's friend just left, with a considerable amount of money for his loyalty and discretion. We need to call Akira and bring him back." Kara was standing silently beside her.

"I just wanted to be free." Philip said. They all turned towards him.

"That was the first thing I've heard him say since shit hit the fan." Todd said.

Philip's tears were streaming down his face. Jack's angry stare loosened up slightly.

"My records say he was released from a mental hospital not too long ago. Seems he has a patchy family history." Jerry said.

"Well, what do we do with him Jack?" Todd asked.

Kara stared at him with indifference. That man shot two holes through the door on top of her, two inches from her face. Still, it wasn't personal even if he did freak out. She understood he wasn't a normal person.

Jack looked away from the prisoner with snot running down his face. Jack's expression was serious.

"I guess we have no other choice."

• • •

"You think you're so smart. I'm sick of your smug face. And keep your trap shut until you can produce all of your goddamn fucking words correctly!"

Akira started swinging the sword with both hands, sending out streaks of fire.

Dmitri didn't move and a blackish purple bubble formed around him. Black lightning surged from it. The flames hit the bubble and instantly evaporated as if they hit arctic water.

"I don't have time to fool around. I will break your will and you will be in a coma until I decide to see if you changed your mind." Dmitri was yelling at this point. It made Akira flinch, but he was glad Dmitri sounded normal at least.

Dmitri held out both his hands and a black streak shot out from the bubble and hit Akira launching him off the roof. His flame sword was gone and the flashlight was now a pile of ashes falling all around him. He barely registered anything as they slipped between his fingers while he plummeted towards the hard imaginary concrete. *I can't lose. There's too much at stake. I can't fail my mother..my father..my friends..*

風

Akira's right hand began glowing blue too. A new symbol. He didn't see it, but he felt it. He managed to lift his feet up towards the sky and tumble backwards so now he was falling face first. He held out both of his hands.

風 火

A flamethrower shot out of his left hand as he was about thirty feet away from the unforgiving ground. It slowed his descent. Then from his right hand he couldn't see it, but he felt energy pass through it. Wind surged around his right arm and hit the ground. He leaned forward and vaulted with the elements he controlled as they hit into the ground. Akira fell about ten feet from the vault and immediately tucked and rolled. He survived the fall, but his tailbone and shoulder hurt from breaking the fall. A car honked at him. He ignored it. *Stupid shadow-faced driver, you're not even real.*

Akira looked up and thought he saw Dmitri watching him from the top of the skyscraper they were just on. A black orb shot up from the rooftop and then quickly expanded like an explosion. Akira reflexively shielded his face. When he moved his arms, the buildings were gone. Tokyo was gone.

He was on an island now. The island was little more than enough to fit an average sized house on. Around the island, waves crashed and rocked the very foundation. Thunder roared and lightning struck rocks sticking out of the water nearby. Akira decided island was the wrong description. It made him think of a beach, what he was on was more of a circle shaped rock formation with sharp pointed rocks at the edges. They acted as barriers to the fierce waves, but they also made Akira feel menacingly cut off from anything off of the island. Dmitri was also on the island now. This was a desolate stone prison in the middle of raging waters.

He opened his eyes. "Now we finish this." Dmitri said. A giant sword appeared in his hands. A broadsword? No. It was bigger than that. It was as big as him! Dmitri's face was blank, and his brown leather duster flowed behind him from the wind.

Dmitri charged at him holding the sharpened weapon with both hands. Akira held up his right hand and shot a current of wind at him.

Dmitri's long coat blew back even harder, as if it wanted to retreat. Even his jet black hair looked like it was going to get torn from his skull, but he persisted step by step. Inching his way closer to the elemental source. Akira used his hand's flamethrower in the vortex of wind he was keeping Dmitri at bay with. Dmitri responded by holding up the giant blade at an angle effectively blocking the fire. Then Akira's energy ran out. He didn't know there was a limit to his powers, in fact, he had forgotten about that long ago when he was shifting in non-combatant's dreams. He didn't consider having a newfound power would drain him even quicker.

No longer suspended by the current of wind, Dmitri shot forward like a Python snatching its victim. Akira was thinking about how impossible it would be to block that blade, and what it would feel like to be dismembered in a dream when the blade slammed into the ground near him. From the ground where the sword struck (if you could call that a sword), a black energy shot up. It swallowed Akira from both sides. It was now a tall dark slab, with flowing energy. Only Akira's arms from the forearm down, his head, and his knees were visible.

Then Dmitri snapped his fingers and the slab split into four pole-like entities six feet apart. Akira was suspended above the ground between the four shadowy pillars by a network of black strings as thick as ropes. He was tangled to the point of complete immobility in the center of the cube.

"This is my shadow prison. See this sword is very special. It's how I trap souls. I only have the power to trap one entirely at a time, so I will leave it here with you my friend. It is already familiar with your family line, because this contained Lin Kishimoto earlier this year. Goodbye, comrade."

Akira tried to move his arms and legs. He could only move his head. He felt the shadow prison's interwoven web sucking his energy dry like a leech on his spirit.

"Shit. Have I grown so weak by power consumption to not have been able to disguise this dispute from others?" Dmitri was the essence of annoyed. He let out a deep sigh.

A little less than a mile away a group of beings appeared. It was all of their first times being in a dream with this many people in it at once. Jack presumed it would not be possible for the average mind and spirit to be able to handle this, but Akira also wasn't the average person. He was on an invisible barrier beside Doctor Abhi Ahmad and Kara Summers. It was levitating them towards the island. Next to them, Todd Rimando was using his ice powers to freeze the angry ocean and create a path towards the island. He had ice in the form of an ice skate at the bottom of his shoes that he used to skate on the path he created.

Dmitri tried to stab the Blade of Shadows into Akira's abdomen to complete the ceremony and lock away Akira's soul, but it was deterred by an unknown force. He placed his foot there to discover it was blocked by a barrier. When he looked back at the rescue party a barrage of icicles went towards him and he blocked them with his sword. Then Jack was above him and swung his fist at where Dmitri stood a second ago before he teleported, then the ground where Jack punched exploded.

When Dmitri reappeared he was on the platform that Doctor had created which now hovered above the island. Doctor was in the center of the platform and Dmitri threw the large blade at him. It defied physics and maintained a circular spin prepared to separate Abhi Ahmad's upper body from his legs. Kara Summers did a side flip and landed on the blade mid-air and then kicked off of it sending it on to the platform where it clanged then skid off of and fell on the island.

Dmitri threw a punch at her and she ducked it, then her nails grew four times their size into sharp animal claws. She tried to impale him but only succeeded in scraping his side as he dodged and sent a kick into her head. As she went flying he teleported behind her and caught her. He placed his hands on her head and prepared to give it a sharp twist when the platform disappeared and they fell twenty feet. Jack and Todd met them mid-air and Jack grabbed Kara from Dmitri's grip while Todd swung his ice blade at him. The ice blade had engulfed Todd's right arm. He cut a bloody gash down Dmitri's arm, and he bragged about Dmitri not being the only one with a large sword but Dmitri grabbed Todd's head and slammed it down into his knee. The quartet all landed at about the same time. Todd got up and circled Dmitri with Kara. Now they mimicked Dmitri's Shadow Prison and surrounded him.

Akira watched in absolute awe. He struggled to keep his eyes open. The Prison reminded him of a time when he was sick. He needed to do homework after missing so many days in school. Lin had given him medicine before she went to work. But after taking it, Akira fought drowsiness to try to stay awake and make up his work. He ended up waking up two hours later drooling on his notebook.

"Cockroaches. Every one of you. I'm most displeased that dis many of you are still alive." He brought his inhuman predator eyes on Jack and turned his body.

Jack met his gaze. "There's still more at HQ. You've failed Noskov."

"I surrender." Dmitri said sullenly. Abhi's eyes opened wide in disbelief. The other three were still ready to move. Then three portals instantaneously opened in front of Dmitri, who looked awkward as he punched through two of them and kicked through the other at the same time.

Dmitri's fists and foot were transported into portals that immediately opened up in front of Jack, Todd and Kara. They all recoiled from the force of the blows. Then Dmitri charged Abhi and started swinging wildly. Abhi kept summoning barriers to block the hits, but his reflexes were gradually slowing. After every few blocks Dmitri would get one hit through Abhi's defenses. Then it was every other. Jack was running to Abhi's aid when Dmitri's last punch went into Abhi's stomach and went out the other end. A surplus of purple light poured out of Abhi's back. Dmitri retired his fist and Abhi's body collapsed. Jack swung a fierce punch at the back of Dmitri's head, but a portal opened up and transported it into Todd's stomach. Unfortunately for Todd, it was an explosive punch and it sent him flying backward with a basketball sized burn on his newly exposed stomach.

"FUCK!" Jack yelled as he pulled his hand from the portal as it almost closed shut on his arm. Dmitri flung a kick into Jack's chest sending him back. Then an elephant charged at Dmitri, who shot a black ball of energy towards it. The elephant transformed back into Kara who was still running, then she transformed into a cheetah and dodged it. It smashed into the pointed rocks behind her with an explosion. She pounced on Dmitri. She attempted to bite his neck but he blocked it with her wrist which she accepted and bit instead.

Jack wanted to see to Abhi but he had to help Akira. He went to one after another of the Prison's pillars touching it with his hands.

It left a blue circle on each. Then he backed away and clenched his palm into a fist and all four pillars exploded.

Kara had transformed into a rhino intent on crushing Dmitri when he teleported away from under her.

Dmitri was underwater next to the island. He had to contemplate his decision. If he stayed he could use up the remainder of his energy to finish them off, but the boy was now without a doubt free. The problem with that, was he'd be at risk of them overpowering his energy and preventing him from retreating. Dmitri had put too much work into everything to leave his life up to a gamble.

Dmitri transcended the physical form he had manifested in Akira's dream, now a mere astral projection, he is intangible and invisible. He flew at a race car-like speed up into the sky as the not-island disappeared into a dot the size of the wound to his pride. He gave that up for his ambition. Once he reached the darkness above, he was transported back into his real body.

They immediately sensed he was gone. Once Jack was sure Akira would be able to return to his body, the MLK exited the dream.

Jack opened his eyes. Todd punched a hole in the wall. Kara looked shattered. She had tears gleaming her eyes. Abhi Ahmad was next to them, cold and dead.

Kristen Pierce kicked open a hotel door to a suite in NYC. She had a Glock in her hands. She hadn't fired a gun since the tragic incident so long ago. The image of her dead ex-boyfriend flashed before her eyes briefly. This time though, she was prepared to use the gun.

Kristen waited until she could sense Dmitri Noskov's energy so she could track him. He was one of the hardest energy's to ever track. When the other's entered Akira's dream (or nightmare one might say) she was finally able to sense that it was in NYC. But the power he held was so immense, she could only limit it to about three square miles. Using the internet, she crossed off all the places in that radius she was sure he wasn't. Then something happened and he grew noticeably weaker. The radius shrank to a mile. Then as she entered a large hotel she suspected the likelihood of finding him in was high, she felt a faint tremor and was actually able to get a mental image of the room he was in. She had no doubt he was using a fake name, so she forced herself to see a door number. It gave her the worst headache of her life, but Sniper found her target.

In the elevator she went. She exited and made quick work of the hallway. Now, Kristen scanned the room. It was empty. She searched the bathroom and closet to no avail. It was too late. Knowing she couldn't have missed him by more than a few minutes, she rushed back to the lobby instead of sulking. When she opened the door to exit the room she was punched in the throat. Dmitri grabbed the gun from her and twisted it while kicking her. She fell backwards into the hotel suite she had just searched. He aimed her own gun at her and a faint smile rose to his face.

CHAPTER 30

November 14th, 2020

Dear Akira,

I know I have failed you as a father. Just as I have failed your mother as a husband. I'm sorry. I have made such tragic mistakes. When I heard your mother was hospitalized I came to New York. I saw her in that bed and it just broke me. I noticed you weren't visiting often. I do not blame you for that, to see someone you love like that--it's just awful, I know. One of the nights I dream shifted into her head. I-spoke to her.. it was truly a nightmare. She was tied up by some black wires or ropes or something, but they were almost alive with hatred and..dear God I swear it was like a hunger..I told Lin everything I told you. She said she knew deep down that I loved her. I told her it was my fault and would you believe what happened next? That woman forgave me. How could someone forgive that? I tried to break her free but I couldn't do anything. Her prison was just too strong.

I contacted the MLK and they discretely had a man named Abhi Ahmad come to the hospital. He helped free her. She was okay again. I was so happy for her. Then I messed up again. I guess you could call it my last mistake. Even now I'm plagued by imperfection and doubt. I thought that you guys would be better off with the dynamic you had. I felt that it was too late to try to be a family again. I fled back to Japan to take the bullseye off of you guys once more. I guess I ran away from my own fear too. I tried leaving the most obvious trace-able path possible to lead Dmitri away, but that didn't work.

The guilt overwhelmed me and I was just happy that she was okay. I couldn't bear to face you. I realize how dumb that was. Dmitri doesn't like to lose. I should have foreseen that as well. At first, I thought he somehow didn't catch me or Abhi like he intended to draw out.. now I think he really did it to force your powers out..please don't shoulder the blame because of this.

Now, I can only do right by you the one way I know how. By giving my powers to you. I love you so much my Son. I'm so sorry things have turned out this way. You deserve better. Well, I think that's enough heart string tugging. I will personally hunt down Dmitri after I give you my strength, and carry the burden of vengeance for both of us. Dmitri was my master once, but I know how to defeat him. I will type you up another letter once I know you're safely back with the MLK. There is no doubt in my mind that you will continue to persevere. My Son is the strongest person I know. Please try to remember me for the father I could have been.

-Your shitty father,
Yakashi Kishimoto

EPILOGUE

NOVEMBER 18TH

KRISTEN WAS SITTING AGAINST A stone wall. The cellar she was in was freezing. She was handcuffed to an old heater that she suspected hadn't worked in years. The cellar was plagued with darkness. She heard a door open. Dmitri Noskov and someone she didn't recognize walked downstairs.

"My boy, I cannot absorb her power yet, but when I learn how we will divide it. You have done as instructed and you will be rewarded with powers beyond your imagination. I'll allow jew to use zhem however zoo wish, but jew will serve me as I call upon you. Do you understand Raymond?"

The boy nodded that he did.

"You know you'll never get away with this," Kristen said. "They'll sense me and follow wherever you go."

"I'm counting on it. We're in Pennsylvania. Let zhem come. I will be waiting. They must be dealt with so my plans can move on."

Ray smiled and waved a gun at her. "Wow you're way more attractive than the bait I've used in the past. But you will squirm just the same." He put his hand on her face and she shrugged it off and tried biting his finger.

"Ooh. Kinky. I like that in a girl."

• • •

231

Akira read over the folded computer document for a third time. He put it back into his wallet. He brought it wherever he went now. The air was frisk. Jack, Todd, Jerry, and Kara walked through a door. As it opened, Akira saw Abhi Ahmad's body on the funeral pyre. He was the only member who was able to have a funeral. They cremated Richard Muchiani, Joan White and Reiner Ulrich. Their deaths were not so easily explained, and they did not have a wife and children.

Akira was so sick of funerals. Sick wasn't an exaggeration either, his stomach actually felt like it was being turned upside down. But he had to be strong.

He put a hand on Jack's bulky shoulder. "We'll find her. And we'll find him. And take him down like he deserves."

Jack nodded. Akira thought he looked like a hitman in his full black suit. "We need to stand together. I've recalled the other members of our organization. We cannot be caught alone. Unfortunately, I was already unable to contact three of those members. Dmitri will pay with his life."

"Count me in." Sid Meyers said while walking up to them. Jack immediately got into a fighting stance but Akira stepped in front of him. "What do you want Sid?"

Sid put something in Akira's hand. Akira raised an eyebrow. "What is this?"

"One hundred dollars. That'll be for room and board for now. I hope your base has a stocked kitchen."

Jack and Akira looked at each other with great disorientation.

• • •

Brent Armstrong, Tyler Walker, and Ian McKinley all shared nightmares on the same night. **A Dark Man** was telling them he needed their help. Two of them wet their beds as **The Dark Man** tormented them into doing his will. The next day their college roommates, siblings, mothers and fathers all found their beds empty.

• • •

Philip Anthony Stone was clean shaved and in a red apron. His name tag read: Andy. It was time for his break. He took off his apron and went to the back. He smiled childishly as he went into the dog kennel. Looking around with great satisfaction and a completely erased and eased mind, he chose which dogs he wanted to let out to play. When Jack, Kristen and Abhi focused their energies real hard, they were able to erase Philip's entire life. Jerry provided him with a new identity and got him a new job. And so he was released, free of Kenneth and bad thoughts and **The Dark Man**. He lived on, not quite able to remember growing up. All he knew was that he had the responsibility of taking care of puppies and finding them good homes.

• • •

Jack was gathering the last of the equipment into the moving truck with the help of Todd and Sid. He didn't fully trust him, but he needed his help badly. The MLK was more desperate than ever.

Jack would be happy to never step foot in the tainted HQ with the vacant doctor's office above it ever again. The door was boarded up and a sign read: **Closed until further notice.**

That boy Akira.. he will lead the MLK. I will make him into a leader. Or I will die trying.

"Uh, sir?"

Jack turned and faced the Professor also known as Jerry.

"You might want to look at this." He gave him Sean Singer's briefcase and Jack mentally kicked himself for forgetting about it.

He rifled through papers and documents inside.

"Holy shit." His eyes were serious and disbelieving at the same time.

"What?" Todd walked over sensing something was up.

"Sean compiled a dossier. A dossier on every rogue Dream Shifter out there. He seems to have thought that Dmitri wasn't working alone, but has recruited partners. There's five others in here. I don't know any of them except-wait. Elijah?"

"Isn't he missing?" Todd asked.

"Apparently not. God damn fucking traitor."

"The stakes just got a lot higher if Dmitri really isn't operating alone anymore. It would explain how he's been able to take out our members across the country. Wait. Jack, this is my dead brother Why would he be in here?" Todd was staring at the paper in utter disbelief.

"Sean died to bring this information to us before it was too late. I'm not sure if everything is accurate, but we'll find out for sure. We will find his ex-girlfriend Kristen for him too. I refuse to fail on this. Dmitri is definitely in contact with others. It makes too much sense. Let's get to work and get out of here. No one else is dying on my watch."

· · ·

Akira was sitting alone in an empty church. He never considered himself religious. His Dad was a Buddhist and his Mom was Agnostic. A tear slipped down his face as he wondered about life on the other side. Was there a heaven? Hell? Purgatory? A realm of spirits? Were his mom and dad watching over him right now?

He used all the logic he could to disprove such things but did he really just want to accept that his mom and dad were dead in the ground? The thought of decomposing bodies slowly turning into skeletal husks left him feeling cold and empty.

"Why do you think people ask us to wake up when we're asleep?"

Akira turned around to the unfamiliar voice.

It was Kara Summers. The quiet blonde girl.

"What do you mean?" He replied.

"If we're not having a nightmare, are we not tranquil and at peace when we rest? Isn't it rude to ask someone to wake up from their peace? Could someone who's comatose be happier than someone who isn't? Or what about when someone is in denial or wallowing in ignorance? We ask them to 'wake up'. We ask that like life itself isn't just one uncontrollable a dream. It passes us by and we can make changes but in the end we're taken away by the currents of life that shape us."

Akira thought that over. He was surprised to hear her say so much.

"Do you believe in God?" she asked.

"I believe there's something. If there is a God I don't think he's anything like the one in the Bible, or any other monotheistic text anyway. He wouldn't answer prayers, shield people from pain or death. No, he'd let things play out. Even if they are the worst things of human nature. He'd let the Holocaust happen, just as he watched the bombs fall on Hiroshima and Nagasaki."

"Is that the kind of God you would want?"

"It doesn't matter," he said swallowing. "I think it's the kind we've got. He or She or It lets us make our own decisions as he has since he created us. He's watched the Church riddle itself in hypocrisy and bigotry. In the end it's up to Us not Him to be strong enough to survive in this world. We drive ourselves forward. To even believe in Him you would need strength on the inside to maintain faith."

She nodded.

"Being a strong person doesn't mean that you don't cry or beat yourself up, a strong person is as simple as someone who has felt loss or inner hatred and still lives and breathes to this day. They keep moving forward no matter what, sometimes without knowing how or why."

"Have you ever wanted to die Akira Kishimoto?"

He seemed ready to answer quickly but then she added: "Like really contemplate killing yourself?"

"There's been more times than I can count where I've wished I didn't have the burden of being a living breathing human being. But no, I have not come close to actually contemplating my own death. It'd be a dishonor to my parents. I think that anyone in this world who has never had a moment in their life where they've thought about death at least once is someone who is not truly alive in this world. Some people move past it, and some don't. All I know is I have a mission and even after it's done I will never give up."

When he finished she leaned forward and kissed him on his cheek. Still an inch away from his face she said: "My mother abandoned me and my sister when I was younger. Our dad had died in an accident. My sister and I found our way into foster care with a mother that cared for us but did not believe that her husband hit us. My sister would sometimes take it out on me too. One day when I was thirteen I simply ran away. You can run away from these people and these problems, but you can't run away from the memories and the mental scars. Life has not been easy for us in the MLK, but we think that might be what awakens our powers; however, I feel a newfound strength emanating from you. This is our first time speaking and I already feel inspired by more than your words.

Stay positive Akira Kishimoto. For some, positivity is all that life is about. I'm certain your parents are proud of you."

"Thank you so much, Kara."

"I also sense something else. You're in love with someone aren't you? I could see it when I kissed your cheek."

"I guess I am, but I don't know." He answered honestly.

Her face said *you either know or you don't*. He decided to elaborate.

"I have a theory. I kind of feel like you can't truly be *in* love with someone, unless they're *in* love with you as well. Loving someone and being *in* love with someone are two entirely different concepts. And if that person isn't *in* love with you, I don't think you can necessarily be *in* love with them anymore. At that point, love becomes past tense. You still care deeply for them, maybe you'd even die for them still if it came down to it, even after an insurmountable amount of time has passed, but life still isn't a fairy tale. I can love someone so much it hurts and that won't change how they feel about me. It becomes acceptance of the inevitable. I think everyone has the capacity to move on. That's how a person can fall in love after their lover died. It just takes time. In a way, I'll always love this girl, but I think I'm coming pretty close to the day that I can love again and that means fall in love as well."

"I see you've thought about this pretty intensely."

"I have, and I still do sometimes. It doesn't matter that much though. I'm a Dream Shifter now, and my duty comes first."

"It'll be interesting to get to know you more Firebird. I'll see you around."

Then Kara was gone. He was in an empty church again.

Heaven or not, Akira knew he wasn't alone. He had friends and allies. But most importantly he had powers other than his dream shifting abilities. He had the power to access all of his memories with his mom, and yes, even his dad when they were younger and cherish them. This was a power anyone who wanted to delve into the happy times shared with a loved one could utilize. If they didn't, the power became a curse. A curse that followed you around and told you *You'll never see them again* and *You'll never be that happy again* and *It's all your fault.* Akira would not be compressed by this curse. His parents did not put him on Earth to live a miserable existence, no matter how rough things got.

His mom died a martyr; his dad a hero. He decided he would live on through both of them and he would never feel alone again. The word *alone* brought Amy back to mind and he shrugged it away. Women were unimportant to him until his work was finished. Dmitri Noskov would be brought to justice. When he succeeded he could live a normal life. He would raise kids, tell them all about their mystical grandparents. Correct the wrongs his dad made. He would stay with his future family no matter what. He would fall in love again.

Akira looked down at his palms which were tattoo-less but when he closed his eyes sometimes, he swore he could feel the energy pulsing through them. *I'll train until I'm the most powerful Dream Shifter the world has ever seen, Dmitri. You better watch out. I'm a Dream Shifter like my father before me and I'm coming for you.*

T H E   E N D !

Keep an eye out for the sequel and finale! Set to wrap up the story in 2018! Thank you <u>so much</u> for reading, it means the world to me that you've gotten this far into my biggest creation to date. I hope the time spent supporting my dream was well worth it.

BONUS: Original poem. Created in the Summer of '16. Copyright 2016. © MCMC

"12/4/12"

> He wanted to throw his cell phone at the wall.
> He wanted to tell the world about the worst moment of all.
> He wanted to go to his bed and stay there until it became a grave..
> He wanted to wake up from a nightmare that made him a slave.
> He wanted to pretend everything was fine, deny it all.
>
> He had just been told his father dropped dead this morning.
> He had seen him forty-eight hours ago, and told him he loved him.

He didn't think it was enough.

He should have stayed.

He wears a cross, only because it was the last thing he was given.

He would have to tell his sister the news.

He had to give someone he loved the worst moment of their life.

He wanted his dad to grab the doorknob and twist it open.

He wanted to put a knife in his chest and twist it open.

Worst of all, he had to be strong. He had to wake up every single day and learn to deal with his father being gone.

He managed. He had no other choice.

He is happier now. He cherishes the memories of the past.

He is living the life his dad would have wanted.

I am He. He is me. 12.4.12, a day, a week, a month, a year I will never forget.

A time I <u>can't</u> forget. I am He.

CPSIA information can be obtained
at www.ICGtesting.com
Printed in the USA
LVOW12s1936181217
560203LV00007B/608/P